"Are you Miss Delia Keller?"

She nodded. "Who are you?"

"My name's Tucker—Jude Tucker, and I'm here because your father wanted me to come see you."

Delia could hardly believe her ears. "My father? You know my father? When will he be here? Oh, I knew he'd be back someday!"

A cloud seemed to pass over his face. "He…he's not coming, Miss Keller. I'm sorry to have to tell you he's dead."

Delia felt the earth shift beneath her feet and she would have fallen if the stranger hadn't steadied her. "What…what happened to my father?" she asked.

"He died mining silver out in Nevada. There was a mine collapse…."

"Thank you for coming to tell me about my father's death, Mr. Tucker."

"But I didn't travel all this way just to inform you of his death. I came to bring you something. You're his only living heir, after all."

"Heir?"

"Well, I suppose *heiress* would be the proper word. Your father died a rich man, Miss Keller. And now all his wealth is yours."

Books by Laurie Kingery

Love Inspired Historical

Hill Country Christmas
The Outlaw's Lady
*Mail Order Cowboy
*The Doctor Takes a Wife
*The Sheriff's Sweetheart
*The Rancher's Courtship
*The Preacher's Bride

*Brides of Simpson Creek

LAURIE KINGERY

makes her home in central Ohio, where she is a "Texan-in-exile." Formerly writing as Laurie Grant for the Harlequin Historical line and other publishers, she is the author of eighteen previous books and the 1994 winner of a Readers' Choice Award in the Short Historical category. She has also been nominated for Best First Medieval and Career Achievement in Western Historical Romance by *RT Book Reviews*. When not writing her historicals, she loves to travel, read, participate on Facebook and Shoutlife and write her blog on www.lauriekingery.com.

Hill Country Christmas
Laurie Kingery

Love Inspired

Recycling programs
for this product may
not exist in your area.

™ LOVE INSPIRED BOOKS

ISBN-13: 978-0-373-78754-8

HILL COUNTRY CHRISTMAS

Copyright © 2008 by Laurie A. Kingery

www.LoveInspiredBooks.com

Printed in U.S.A.

Delight thyself also in the Lord; and
he shall give thee the desires of thine heart.
—*Psalms* 37:4

To the beautiful Hill Country of Texas, the place my soul feels most at home this side of Heaven, and to all my relatives in Texas, especially Aunt Joann.

Chapter One

Llano Crossing, Texas—August 1867

"He was a good man, Miss Delia. He's certainly in the arms of Jesus now."

"God rest his soul."

"God bless you in your time of sorrow, Miss Delia."

The hillside that had been covered in the golden glory of a Texas spring when Reverend McKinney had begun to fade—primroses and coreopsis, gaillardia and red-centered Indian blanket, punctuated here and there by bluebonnets lingering from the month before—was now, after the summer sun had done its work, sere and brown. It seemed a fitting backdrop for the unrelieved black garments of the figures in the valley who stood around the deep rectangular hole into which a coffin had just been lowered.

Sorrow didn't begin to name the endless depth of Delia's grief. Her grandpa had been the only element of stability she had experienced in her eighteen years of life, and now he was gone.

Another voice intruded on her thoughts. "I'm sorry

for your loss, Miss Delia. If you need anything, you have but to let me or any of my family know. Reverend McKinney was a pillar of this community, and we would not want his granddaughter to be in need."

Under the black brim of her bonnet, Delia Keller raised her eyes to the speaker. "Thank you, Charles. I appreciate it." If she had hoped for more from the mayor's son, she made sure her face did not give her away. She didn't want Charles Ladley's pity, if that was all she could have from him.

The tight starched neckline of her borrowed bombazine mourning dress threatened to choke her.

Oh, Heavenly Father, what am I to do now?

A few of the ladies began to drift away from the gravestones toward the makeshift tables laden with covered baskets that were spread out under the live oak trees between the small church and the cemetery. Soon, Delia knew, they would have a hearty dinner spread out for those who had attended the funeral—ham and fried chicken, black-eyed peas, freshly baked biscuits, chocolate cake and pecan pralines. There would be pitchers of lemonade and cold tea. As the chief mourner, Delia would be expected to partake, sample and praise each lady's culinary offering.

The thought of putting so much as a crumb in her mouth made nausea roil in her stomach. The noon heat beat down on her head through her bonnet. She couldn't do it.

She'd thought everyone had left her side and she was alone at the grave site, but now Delia felt a gentle touch on her wrist. "Miss Keller, are you all right?"

It was Reverend Calhoun from Mason, who had

kindly come to conduct the funeral, since Llano Crossing was now preacherless.

She looked away from the concern in his old eyes, afraid she would dissolve into tears but knowing it was safe to confide in him.

"What am I going to do, Reverend Calhoun? My whole life was taking care of my grandpa."

He gave her an understanding smile. "You needn't decide that today, my dear," he reminded her. "You've suffered a loss, a grievous loss, and it'll take a while to find your feet. But the Lord will show you a way."

Delia blinked, wiping away a tear that managed to escape from her eyes. She had no patience with platitudes this morning. "The town will be finding a new preacher, and he'll need to live in the parsonage—where am I to go? I have no money, no employment…" *No beau,* she added to herself. She wouldn't be going to live in the beautiful white house Charles Ladley would build someday for his bride, and the worst thing was, she didn't even know why not.

"The Lord will reveal all that to you, Miss Keller," the preacher assured her, confidence mingled with compassion in his deep, resonant voice, "in the fullness of time. He takes care of the birds in the air and the lilies of the field, you know. Now come—it looks as if the good ladies of Llano Crossing have prepared a nice meal for you." Nodding toward the tables under the trees, he said, "Why don't we—"

"I…I don't think I can stay for it," she said quickly, keeping her gaze on the toes of her high-button boots, but away from the grave. "I just…I just want to go back to the parsonage and lie down." *While I still can lie down there—and try to imagine what I'm going to do.*

"Nonsense, child, you need to put some food in your stomach, and take heart from the others who loved Reverend McKinney," urged his wife, a comfortable-looking gray-haired woman who had returned to her husband's side. "You'll feel better after you've eaten a bite, I'm sure."

Delia did not want to argue with her, and fortunately the visiting preacher made it unnecessary.

"Mrs. Calhoun, can't you see the girl is pale as a wilted primrose? I'm sure she knows what's best for her. There's bound to be plenty of food left, and we can bring her a plateful to tempt her appetite after she's had a nap. Miss Delia, we'll see you later," Reverend Calhoun said with finality. A look passed between husband and wife.

"All right, Mr. Calhoun, I'll walk with her," Mrs. Calhoun said, to Delia's dismay. "You go say the blessing so everyone can start eating. I'll be back in just a few minutes."

Placing an arm around Delia's waist, as if she feared the girl might swoon without it, Mrs. Calhoun started forward.

The parsonage sat some fifty yards down the road from the church. If she wasn't allowed to walk home by herself, Delia figured that at least, once there, she would insist she could find her way to her bedroom without any help. She would be alone in minutes.

They had nearly reached the gate that let out onto the dusty road when they spotted the horse and rider trotting toward them from the west, trailed by a swirl of dust.

"If he's coming for the funeral, he's a little late," Mrs. Calhoun said with a sniff.

"Oh, I don't imagine he is," Delia said. She thought everyone who had ever attended the Llano Crossing Church had been present for the funeral service. The church had been filled to bursting, with folks overflowing out onto the steps. "Probably just another cowboy coming into town to enjoy Saturday night."

Mrs. Calhoun pursed her mouth. "And tomorrow all he'll have is an aching head to show for his month's wages."

As the rider drew nearer, however, Delia began to doubt he'd come from any of the many nearby ranches. In back of the saddle were bulging saddlebags, a blanket roll and a rifle. The silver buckskin he rode was wet to his hocks, as if he'd just crossed the Llano at one of its deeper points upstream, rather than waiting to cross at the town that bore the name of the bridge that spanned the river.

He reined the horse to a walk a few yards away; then, as he reached them, he halted the horse with a soft *whoa*. He laid a finger on the broad brim of his hat in an automatic gesture.

"Ladies, is Llano Crossing up ahead?"

His voice was gravelly and rough, as if it had been unused for a long while. His eyes, which were studying her with a frankness she had never been subjected to, were the glacial gray-blue color of a wolf's. She felt herself shiver as if the sudden chill breeze of a norther had blown upon her spine.

Out of the corner of her eye, Delia saw Mrs. Calhoun give a rigid nod. "Just around the bend in the road."

"And would a traveler find a hotel there where he could pass the night?" he asked, without taking those wolfish eyes off Delia.

She saw Mrs. Calhoun stiffen even more before she replied, "He would, if he were a law-abiding, respectable sort."

Delia saw the threat of a smile cross the stranger's face like slow heat lightning. He looked as if he would ask something more of Delia, then apparently thought better of it. "Much obliged, ma'am," he said, touching his hat brim yet again, his gaze drifting over to Mrs. Calhoun just long enough to be polite.

The corner of his mouth twitched as if it wanted to turn upward; then, as if noticing the somber hue of Delia's black dress, it resumed its previous thin line as he nodded and touched the buckskin with his boot heel. "Ladies," he murmured, and once he and the horse were a few yards from them, he nudged the horse into an easy lope.

Mrs. Calhoun sniffed again. "Well! He might have shown some respect."

Delia glanced at her, surprised at the indignation in the woman's voice. "He touched his hat."

"I mean to our mourning, my dear! Why, he was staring at you like a wolf set loose in a sheep pen!"

Since a wolf was the very creature she had been reminded of also, Delia blinked in surprise. Mrs. Calhoun was probably expecting too much of the man, though, if she thought that the stranger would give a long, involved condolence speech merely because the two of them were dressed in black.

"A saddle tramp, I shouldn't wonder," Mrs. Calhoun muttered disapprovingly. "There are so many of them drifting through ever since the war. Like tumbleweeds."

Delia was sure Mrs. Calhoun was right, but she didn't want to encourage the woman to linger, so she remained silent as they reached the low, crumbling rock wall that separated the parsonage yard from the road.

"Thank you for your kindness, Mrs. Calhoun. I'll be fine," Delia said as she stepped onto the flower-bordered pathway that led up to the white frame house. "I'll see you later."

The preacher's wife took the hint after giving Delia one last look of concern.

"All right, if you're certain you don't want someone to sit with you," Mrs. Calhoun said uncertainly, but then she started walking briskly back in the direction they had come, as if afraid the other mourners would devour everything on the tables before she got back to them. She paused only long enough to call back over her shoulder, "Pastor Calhoun and I will be quiet as mice when we return, in case you're still napping. Get some rest, dear."

Delia was sure she wouldn't so much as close her eyes, but at least she had freed herself from the suffocating, if well-meant, sympathy.

She was awakened sometime during the night by Reverend Calhoun's sonorous snoring coming from her grandpa's former room down the hall. Padding quietly to the kitchen at the back of the one-story frame house, she found that her visitors had been as good as their word and had left her a delicious supper of fried chicken, biscuits and pralines from the funeral dinner. She ate, and then waited for dawn, praying some answers about her future would arrive with the sun.

"I don't feel right about leaving so soon," Mrs. Calhoun fretted two days later, after they had breakfasted on eggs Delia had collected from her grandpa's—she still thought of them as her grandpa's—hens. "Why, this girl is a bereaved orphan! It isn't decent to leave her like this, Mr. Calhoun!"

"I'm not *actually* an orphan, Mrs. Calhoun," Delia informed her. "My father is traveling in the west. I'm sure he'll be home one of these days soon." She'd said these words so many times before. "If he'd known about Grandpa's illness, he'd have been home already, I'm sure," she added, hoping it sounded like she believed what she was saying.

Mrs. Calhoun, who'd been in the act of levering her bulk up from the chair, turned to her. "Now dear, I know that must be a comforting thought, but your neighbor, Mrs. Purvis, told me you and your grandpa had heard nothing from your father since he left! I'll pray he returns home, but don't you think he would have done so already if he was going to?" Her voice was so pityingly compassionate that Delia wanted to grind her teeth.

"Papa *will* be home someday," she said. "I know he will. After Mama died, he got itchy feet, as Grandpa called it."

"He could've gone to fight alongside our boys in gray," Mrs. Calhoun said, disapproval plain on her face.

Delia didn't bother to tell her that if her father had been inclined to be a soldier at all, he probably would've worn blue. Feelings about the War Between the States still ran high in these parts.

"He said he'd gotten married so young that he'd never had the chance to see the West. He promised he was going to be home just as soon as he struck it rich."

She hated the way her voice quavered as she remembered the hurt she had felt as she watched him ride off seven years ago. *Why was I not enough for you, Papa?*

Mrs. Calhoun tsk-tsked. "'For the love of money is the root of all evil,'" she quoted sententiously. She looked as if she was going to say something more.

"If I have not charity, love profiteth me nothing," the old preacher paraphrased, giving his wife a quelling look before turning to Delia. "I pray your faith will soon be rewarded, child."

Delia tried to assume a carefree expression. "I'll be fine, Mr. and Mrs. Calhoun. Really, I will. If I need anything, the Purvises said just to ask."

She wished the preacher and his wife had gone yesterday, but since yesterday was Sunday, Pastor Calhoun felt an obligation to conduct the regular worship service at the Llano Crossing Church. Who knew how long it would be before the town would have another preacher?

It had seemed so strange—*wrong,* even—for someone else to be standing in the pulpit in her grandpa's place, speaking about God. Reverend Calhoun wasn't a bad preacher, and he certainly knew his Bible, but he didn't have Delia's grandfather's dry humor. Nor did he place his pocket watch on the pulpit as Reverend McKinney had done so he'd know when it was time to close. It had taken several pointed looks from a deacon before Reverend Calhoun had ceased his flow of oratory and said the benediction.

Afterward, of course, Mrs. Calhoun hadn't felt right about traveling on the Sabbath, so Delia had been obliged to endure the woman's well-meant but stifling clucking over her and insistence that she knew best what Delia ought to be doing at every moment for the rest of that endless day.

"Mrs. Calhoun, if we leave now we'll be home before supper," Preacher Calhoun said now, laying his napkin aside and rising from the table. "Miss Delia has assured us she will write if she needs anything, or better yet, have someone ride with her up the road to Mason for a long visit, won't you, my dear?"

Delia assured them she would.

"Perhaps I should just help Delia with these dishes." Mrs. Calhoun fretted, waving a plump hand over the crumbs of toast and yellow flecks of egg that adorned the plates. "It's not Christian to eat and dash off like that, Mr. Calhoun."

The preacher raised eyes Heavenward as if asking for patience. "And then you'll say it's too close to dinnertime. No, Mrs. Calhoun, we are leaving this very minute. Delia won't mind. Goodbye, Delia, and thank you for your hospitality in this trying time. Please know I'll be praying for you every day."

"Thank you, Reverend Calhoun," Delia said, keeping her eyes downcast lest his wife discern just how relieved she was that they were leaving. Having guests could be exhausting in the best of times. Now she was eager to be alone with her thoughts and not have the constant duty of being pleasant and hospitable.

She picked up the picnic basket she had packed with the remains of the ham, several slices of bread and some butter she'd wrapped in a cold, wet cloth, and she walked to the door before Mrs. Calhoun could think of any further reason to dally.

Chapter Two

Reverend Calhoun's fondness for sweet tea had left Delia with only an inch or two of sugar in the bottom of the rose-sprigged china sugar bowl, she discovered when she sat down to drink her coffee.

Fortunately, the hens had provided eggs she could bring into town to sell at the general store, then buy sugar with some of the money Mr. Dean paid her, and have a few coins to put aside for another day. But what was she going to do when she needed a sizable sum? If the windmill broke and she had to have it repaired, for example? And she had assumed it might take some time for the town to find a new pastor. If the perfect candidate was available, Llano Crossing's time without a preacher would be brief—leaving Delia without a home. She would have to be able to pay rent somewhere.

Her grandpa had never been a great one for saving, believing that the Lord would meet his needs, even if he gave his meager salary to any down-on-his-luck tramp who showed up at the door. The Lord had always come through, often in the guise of one of the church members who brought them a side of beef or a bushel of peaches. But she couldn't count on that to continue, now that her grandpa had gone on to his heavenly reward.

The Lord helps those who help themselves, she reminded herself. She'd better look into getting a job while she was in town, so when the time came she could afford to put another roof over her head, even if it was just a room at Mrs. Mannheim's boardinghouse. Perhaps Mr. Dean could use another clerk at the general store, or Mrs. Jackson might need an assistant cook at the hotel. If worst came to worst, she could offer to clean and cook for Mrs. Mannheim in exchange for her room and board, though she had heard the German widow was an exacting woman who preferred to do everything herself. Or she could write to Reverend Calhoun and have him check into employment opportunities in Mason, as he'd offered during his stay.

She hoped, however, that she wouldn't have to leave Llano Crossing. She'd been living here ever since she was eleven, when her father had brought her here as his wife was dying.

Taking a minute to gaze at herself in the cracked mirror, which hung in her room, she made sure the bow of the black bonnet had even loops and her thick brown curly hair was still enclosed in a neat knot on the back of her neck. Black washed out her complexion, making her even paler than she was, but the walk to town ought to bring a little color to her cheeks. In the meantime, she pinched them then picked up her egg basket and went out the door.

Intent on her thoughts, eyes on the path before her, she almost opened the rusted gate into the horse standing in the shade of the oak tree at the roadside.

"Oh! I didn't know anyone was there!" she said, her hand falling from the gate as she took a step back.

It was the stranger she'd seen yesterday, the one who'd asked directions into town.

He touched the brim of his hat once again. "Yes, ma'am, you did seem like your mind was elsewhere. I didn't mean to startle you."

"You...you didn't," she lied, though she knew it was plain as punch he had. He had changed since yesterday; if not for the fact that he was riding the same horse, she might not have recognized him. He had the same wintry gray-blue eyes, but he'd obviously used his evening at the hotel to bathe and shave and have his clothes laundered—or perhaps they were new ones, bought from the mercantile.

Delia was afraid she was staring.

"Can I...can I help you?" She was used to unknown people showing up at her grandpa's door, looking for a handout, or perhaps just spiritual advice, but she didn't want to tell this wolfish stranger she was alone here. "I'm afraid the reverend isn't available right now...."

"I know. Are you Miss Delia Keller?"

She nodded, feeling her heart pounding in her ears. How had he known her name? What did he want?

"I heard about your grandpa's unfortunate passing when I got to town," the stranger said. "I reckon that was his funeral you were leaving yesterday. Had I known who you were, Miss Keller, I would have stopped to talk to you yesterday, not ridden on past." His voice was deep, like the bottom of a slowly flowing Texas river.

Delia blinked. "Who...who are you?"

The man dismounted before he spoke and dropped

the reins to the ground. The buckskin seemed used to this action and merely dropped his head to crop at the grass that grew lushly in the shade by the fence.

As the man turned back to her, she got a true measure of his height. Somehow he was even taller than he had seemed on horseback. He would have easily overtopped her grandpa, who had become stooped in his old age, and was probably taller than her father, whom she hadn't seen since the top of her head reached only to his elbow. The stranger would probably have had to duck to enter her house—not that she was even thinking of inviting him in!

He seemed to sense her qualms, for he held his ground and removed his broad-brimmed hat, revealing a headful of raven-dark hair. "Miss Keller, my name's Tucker—Jude Tucker—and the reason I'm here is that your father wanted me to come by and see you."

She could hardly believe her ears, and her eagerness had her rushing forward as fast as she had been backing up. "My father? You know my father? Is he coming? When will he be here? Why didn't he come with you? Oh, I *knew* he'd be back someday!"

A cloud seemed to pass over Tucker's face, and he put out a hand, not to touch her but to stop the flow of her words.

"He…he's not coming, Miss Keller. I'm sorry, I should have made that clear right off. I—I'm sorry to have to be the one to tell you he's dead."

Delia felt the earth shift beneath her feet as if she had been whirled around a dozen times and let loose. She would have fallen if the stranger hadn't put out a hand just then to steady her.

"Easy there," Jude Tucker murmured, his touch gentle. "You're white as bleached bones, Miss Keller. Why don't we step up onto your porch and sit down on those chairs? I've given you a shock, ma'am, but I reckon you'll be wanting to hear the rest once you've had a few moments to think."

She didn't remember giving permission, but with his hand on her elbow, he guided her up the three steps and settled her into the rocker that had been her grandpa's favorite place to while away an evening. He watched as she untied her black bonnet and set it on the small table between them.

"Is there a pump around back? Could I fetch you a cup of water?" Tucker asked.

His voice seemed to come from a long way off, and Delia had to force herself to make sense of his words before she could answer him. "A pump? Water? No... That is, yes, there's a pump, but no, I don't want any...."

Then, as the result of years of modeling herself after her grandpa, who'd never done the least thing without thinking of other people first, she added, "Oh, but feel free to help yourself, if you're thirsty. There's a cup hanging by a string from the pump."

He looked surprised. "It's mighty nice of you to be askin' at such a time, ma'am. Perhaps I'll do that, after I've told you about why your father sent me to see you."

"What...what happened to my father?" she said, swallowing past a lump in her throat, her eyes burning as she struggled to focus on the stranger.

Jude Tucker looked down at the hat he held between his long, tanned fingers. "He died mining silver out in Nevada, Miss Keller," he said.

When she said nothing, merely waited, he looked up at her, then went on.

"You probably know they struck silver out there in '59, long before he got there, but your father discovered a new mother lode nearby. I'd been helping him mine it. He'd been lucky—luckier than anyone's been since the Comstock Lode. He'd been saying he was going to head back to Texas, but before he could there was a mine collapse. I'd gone to town for supplies with the wagon, and he'd gotten pinned under a couple of big beams for several hours. He…"

Tucker paused, then seemed to think better of what he was going to say. His eyes shifted toward the road, but Delia could tell he wasn't really seeing anything. He was remembering.

"It was clear he was in a bad way when I got there. I pulled the beams off him. I was all for trying to get him to the doctor, but he wouldn't go. He told me he knew he was dying. There probably wasn't anything the sawbones could've done anyway, and the ride would have killed him. He told me just to let him lie there so he could use the moments he had left to tell me where to find you, Miss Keller. He was gone just a few minutes after that."

Delia felt a hot knife of regret stab her. If only her father hadn't been so restless—if only he hadn't felt that need to go seek his fortune. He'd be alive today, and she wouldn't have had to grow up without a father. Mrs. Calhoun had been unknowingly right when she'd quoted that verse from the Bible. The love of money had certainly been the root of evil for Will Keller.

"And now you have," she said, remembering her manners. "It was good of you to come so far, Mr. Tucker, to tell me about my father's death. I…I don't have any way to repay you for your trouble."

Something shifted in the depths of those steely eyes. "You're welcome, but I…didn't come all this way just to inform you of his death. I came to bring you something. You're his only living heir, after all."

"Heir?" Once again, it was as if he was speaking a foreign language.

His lips curved upward slightly. "Well, I suppose *heiress* would be the proper word, ma'am. In my saddlebags I have a certificate from the bank in Carson City that you can have transferred to your bank here in town."

"Certificate? What do you mean?"

"Your father had already mined quite a lode of silver before anyone—anyone besides me, that is—got wind that he'd struck such a big vein. He converted it to cash and put that in the bank. He died a rich man, Miss Keller. And now all his wealth is yours."

He'd been afraid that the news might cause her to faint for real this time. Jude watched, ready to catch her, as the heavy dark lashes flew up and surprise siphoned the blood once more from her cheeks, but Delia Keller remained upright.

A soft gasp escaped her lips. "Rich? *My* father? And he left it all to *me?*"

Her incredulity at being the sole beneficiary surprised him in turn. "You *were* his only child, Miss Keller. Who else should he leave it to?"

"I…I don't know," she stammered in bewilderment. "As long as he'd been gone from here, I thought it possible that he might…well, have married again. Maybe even started a new family somewhere."

Jude wished his friend were alive again, if only for a moment, so he could upbraid him for deserting his responsibility to his only child and making this beautiful woman doubt her importance to her father. Compared to that, even the thousands of dollars Will Keller had left her were fool's gold.

"Or he could have left it to you, his partner." She'd been looking down at her lap, but now he found those green eyes trained right on him.

Jude found himself unable to meet her frank regard. "I...I wasn't his partner," he explained. "I just worked for him. He found the silver all by himself. He gave me plenty for traveling expenses, Miss Keller. That was enough."

"You could have kept the certificate and claimed you couldn't find me. No one would have been the wiser."

Those eyes seemed to bore right through him, straight to his soul.

"No, I couldn't have," he said, wondering what Delia Keller looked like clothed in some color other than black. Green perhaps, to match her eyes. Now, that would be a picture. "Besides, what would I do with so much money? I go where the wind takes me."

"You're a drifter?"

It was phrased as a question, but it wasn't one. Jude knew she had sized him up when he'd asked for directions yesterday—or if she hadn't, the sour-faced woman next to her had done it for her.

"You don't want to settle down somewhere, Mr. Tucker? Put down roots, make a home?"

He had to quell her inquiries before he ended up saying more than he meant to. Jude gave her a direct look, a look that was a little too bold, a look that said she didn't know him nearly well enough to be asking such a personal thing.

"The question is, what are *you* going to do with it, Miss Keller? That's what you need to be thinking of."

He saw the flush sweep up her neck and into her cheeks and knew she'd gotten the message he intended.

"Oh! I...I suppose you're right...." A parade of emotions played across her face as he watched, from astonishment to thoughtfulness to amusement.

"Well, this *does* change things, doesn't it? I was on the way to town to sell my eggs so I'd have enough to buy sugar, and I thought while I was there I'd see about getting a job. I thought I'd better start saving some money for when the new preacher arrived and I had to find a new place to live."

He laughed. "You won't have to do that now, Miss Keller."

She smiled, a smile of dawning confidence. "No, I won't, will I? I...I can buy a house if I want to, can't I?"

He nodded, amused. She really had no idea, just yet, of just how wealthy she was. "Miss Keller, with the wealth represented by that certificate, there, you can have a house built to your exact specifications. It could be the biggest house in Llano Crossing, if you wanted. Or you could move anywhere you like."

"I—I see," she breathed. "Well! That does give me something to think about, doesn't it?"

A gleam flashed across those clear green eyes. Delia Keller looked as if she'd thought of something very satisfying. Jude wondered for a moment what it was.

"What do you suggest I do first, Mr. Tucker?" she asked.

"You said you were going to town. You should still go, and right away. Get that certificate into the bank safe before you tell anyone—and I mean *anyone*—about it."

She looked startled at his sudden grimness.

"Mr. Tucker, this is a small town, full of good people, not swindlers and cardsharps. It's not as if someone would snatch it out of my hand," she protested.

"You asked my opinion, Miss Keller," he reminded her. "All I'm saying is, go to the bank first, before you speak to anyone about what I've told you. After that, you can sit up on the roof of the town hall and call out the news from there, if you've a mind to."

Jude could see his blunt words had splashed cold water on her bubbling excitement, which was as he'd intended. A little caution would serve her well.

"Very well. I'm sure it's good advice," she said. "Would you suggest that I not mention it to anyone afterward, either? Other than the bank president, I mean—he'll have to know because I'll have to tell him how I came by this certificate. But people will guess something has happened when I start looking for property...." Her voice trailed off and she looked at him uncertainly.

He managed not to laugh at her naiveté. "I think you'll find that word will get around as if it had wings, Miss Keller. Be very careful. You're going to find that the way people have treated you is about to change. Don't trust everything that people say to you."

She studied him for a long moment and looked as if she were about to ask him how he knew so much. But apparently, after the way he had responded to her other personal question, she decided against it, for she just nodded.

"I'll do as you suggest," she said, rising. "Perhaps

you would accompany me, Mr. Tucker? The least I could do would be to buy you dinner at the hotel afterward, after the distance you've come to inform me of this…this astonishing change in my situation," she said. She'd have to ask the bank president for an advance of cash in order to pay for the meal, of course, but that shouldn't be a problem.

Chapter Three

He laughed, but this time it was a mirthless sound that stung her pride. "Miss Keller, you're a rich woman now, but you still need to be careful of what people will say. Being seen with a stranger—especially being seen dining with me—would not be good for your reputation."

She hadn't thought of that, but was determined to persuade him. "If I introduce you—if I explain that you were my father's friend and came here to inform me of his death—I'm sure no one would think ill of it."

He shook his head. "That wouldn't make a difference," he said. "In fact, it might make things worse. No, you'd do better to pretend we never met—other than yesterday, of course, when I asked for directions. That wasn't exactly a formal introduction."

"But what will you do? Where will you go from here?" she asked. She'd wanted to hear more from this man about her father—and, if she were honest with herself, she wanted to spend a little more time in the company of Jude Tucker, though she couldn't have said why. There was just something about him. Perhaps it was only because he had brought the news that had just changed her life.

For a moment, he looked as if he was going to ask her why she cared enough to ask. Then he said, shrugging, "I don't know. I'm a fair enough carpenter.... I'll probably stick around town awhile, do some odd jobs to build up a stake so I can go back out West."

"It's honest work," she murmured.

"It'll take a long time to earn enough that way."

"If you're in that much of a hurry, maybe you should rob the bank," she suggested tartly.

"The same bank you're about to go to? Not a very wise suggestion, Miss Keller."

She stiffened at his teasing. "I'm just going to take these eggs back into the kitchen, and then I must be going," she said, going to pick up the basket she had left by the gate. "Good day, Mr. Tucker. Thank you for your kindness in coming, and for your honesty in bringing me my father's legacy."

"Goodbye, Miss Keller," he said, donning his hat again and pulling it low, so his eyes were in shadow. "Remember, if you see me around town, we haven't met."

His unnecessary reminder, and his failure to acknowledge her thanks, irritated her. "That won't be a problem," Delia said, her voice curt.

Tucker had been compassionate in the way he'd informed her of her father's death, but after that he'd done nothing but make her feel like a gullible innocent. Very well! She had tried to show her gratitude and he'd virtually thrown the offer back in her face—even made her feel that, by offering, she had seemed a little forward.

He was gone when she came back out, and she resolved to put Jude Tucker from her mind. With any luck, she wouldn't encounter him again, and she could concentrate on the message he had brought, rather than the messenger.

Her father was dead. It was strange, Delia mused as she walked down the road, but after the initial stab of grief, she felt…nothing. Perhaps, since he'd been gone without a word for so long, he had been dead to her anyway. Of course, Delia hoped he hadn't suffered and that, in the time between the accident and Tucker's return to the mine, her father had thought to pray.

He had believed in Jesus, Delia remembered. She recalled times he'd listened to her prayers and read her stories from the Bible. But that had been before her mother's passing, which had set the wanderlust loose in his soul so badly that he couldn't bide at home and be a father to her.

Delia winced, remembering now how often she'd expressed anger toward her father when talking to her grandpa.

"Delia, darlin'," she could hear him say in his drawling voice, rusty with age, "it's plumb understandable and human that you feel that way, but you'd do better to pray for him, for his safety and his quick return. Let's read that story in the Bible about the Prodigal Son. Maybe your papa will be just like that, and we'll have a feast to celebrate."

Surely it was a sin to be angry toward the dead. Her father was no longer capable of coming back to her.

But what about my prayers, God? I prayed for Papa's safety and his return, and You let him die in a mine collapse, hundreds of miles away.

"God always hears us, child," she could hear her

grandpa say, as clearly as if he had been right there by her, "but sometimes his answer is no. And sometimes we won't ever know—this side of Heaven, at least— why that's so."

And now that I'm a rich woman, it's too late for me to help Grandpa with my money. How wonderful it would have been if she could have used some of it to buy him some comfort in his old age. She'd have insisted he move into her new house with her, or if he hadn't been willing, she could have at least had the tumbledown old parsonage fixed so that its roof no longer leaked and its walls were freshly painted.

He'd probably have insisted she send the money to missionaries in Africa instead, Delia mused, and found her cheeks wet with tears. She could mourn her grandpa, even if she couldn't feel deep sorrow for her father.

The town of Llano Crossing lay just around a wooded bend from its church and parsonage. Jude Tucker tied his horse among the cottonwoods that lined the curve of the river and followed Delia on foot, keeping his distance among the trees so she wasn't aware of him. He was pleased to see that true to his instruction, she went straight to the bank without dillydallying to chat with any of the handful of townsfolk who greeted her in passing.

He hadn't expected Delia Keller to be a beauty. Nothing her father had told him while they worked shoulder to shoulder in the mine, or later, when Will lay dying in the wreckage of that same mine, had prepared Jude for those large green eyes, that slender, slightly long nose, that rosebud of a mouth, all set in a heart-shaped face with a faint sprinkling of freckles. He supposed that when Will had last seen his daughter before heading West, Delia had been at that awkward, coltish stage that many girls go through just before being transformed into beauties.

He doubted that Delia even knew she was pretty. There was something unawakened, unaware in those clear green eyes. Her gaze had been direct when she had invited him to escort her to the bank and to buy him dinner. Perhaps it was because he had just told her of her father's death, but Jude was used to women who knew how fluttering their eyelashes just so at a man would get them their way.

There was also a total lack of vanity in the ugly high-necked black mourning dress she wore. Maybe the dress was borrowed. He had known women who looked striking in black, but Delia wasn't one of them. The harsh, flat hue leeched the color from her cheeks—and yet somehow she was still beautiful.

Now that she was wealthy beyond most women's dreams, though, she could at least improve the quality of her mourning. She could buy dresses in finer fabrics, black mourning jewelry and fetching hats to replace that ugly poke bonnet....

Better clothing, along with her change in status from an impoverished orphan to a wealthy heiress, would draw men like flies. He hoped Delia Keller had some shrewdness to go with her comeliness, or she'd find herself the victim of some smooth-talking fortune-hunter who'd treat her to a whirlwind courtship and then, as her husband, exert sole control over the money her father had wanted to benefit his daughter.

Lord, protect her. Make her as wise as a serpent yet harmless as a dove, as the Good Book says.

Will Keller had suggested that Jude be the one to marry and protect her, right after he had struck it rich. "You should go to Llano Crossing and marry my daughter, Tucker. She's a sweet girl, my Delia. You'd be good for one another."

He'd scoffed at Will for saying it. "Will, what does your daughter need with the likes of me? Besides, we'll probably never meet. You'll go home one day, now that you've made your fortune, and I'll keep looking for a rich claim of my own."

"Or a rich widow," Will had joked, wiping the sweat out of his eyes.

Jude had only shook his head. He was done with widows—especially those who claimed to be widows who really weren't at all. He'd settle down with a woman someday, he supposed. He wasn't a good enough man to always resist the clamoring wants of his body forever. But he certainly wasn't worthy of an innocent girl like Delia, a preacher's granddaughter. Not after Nora.

"This is extraordinary news, Miss Keller," Amos Dawson, the bank president, said, laying aside his wire-rimmed spectacles and the certificate Delia had shown him, and crossing his arms over his considerable paunch. "You're saying you had no idea that your father had amassed such a fortune?"

"Yes," she murmured, feeling uneasy at his staring. His black beady eyes reminded her of her grandpa's old rooster—right before the bossy bird tried to peck at her legs. "I—I mean no, I had no idea. We—my grandpa and I—hadn't heard from him in years, you see. We didn't even know if he was alive or dead."

"How did you get hold of this document? Did it come in the mail?"

Delia wanted to say it had, to avoid questions about Jude Tucker, since he had cautioned her not to claim any acquaintance with him. But it would be easy enough for Dawson to check with the gossipy postmaster of the little town, who knew who was receiving mail from where and didn't mind telling anyone who asked.

"I… That is, the man who had been working for him brought it to me."

Dawson continued to scrutinize until Delia felt a flush creeping up the scratchy neckline of her dress.

"We'll have to telegraph the bank in Nevada to verify its authenticity," he said at last.

Delia felt foolish. The bank couldn't just assume the certificate was real and start issuing her funds based on it. The document could be a clever fraud.

"I…I assumed as much," she said, trying to sound like a woman of the world. "Naturally."

Dawson seemed pleased with her composure. "We'll do so immediately, I assure you, Miss Keller. I would imagine it will take a few days to obtain an answer— but during that time, I regret that I can't…that is, the *bank* cannot act on the basis of this document."

Delia nodded. "I understand completely," she said, rising. It wasn't a problem. She had been poor when she woke up this morning, and she could go on pinching pennies and doing without for a few more days. She only wished she had brought those eggs after all—now she was going to have to walk back to the house and get them or do without sugar in her tea another day.

Dawson rose also. "Assuming this certificate is authentic, Miss Keller, this is very exciting news, isn't it? Just wait until the word gets out!"

Delia felt a prickle of alarm dance up her spine. He was practically clapping his hands together with glee, as if he wanted to be the first to spread the news. "I hope I can rely on your discretion, Mr. Dawson. I...I wouldn't want to be the subject of speculation...especially before the certificate has been proved genuine."

Dawson coughed and took a step back, and his features smoothed out as if an invisible hand had wiped all expression from his face. "Of course not, Miss Keller. Rest assured. But only imagine the possibilities of what you will be able to do with such a sum! The bank will be pleased to be of any assistance to you that you would require."

"Fine. Please let me know when you've received confirmation. Good afternoon, Mr. Dawson."

She swept out, disturbed at the complete transformation in the way the bank president treated her once he had heard the news. No wonder Grandpa had never had much use for Amos Dawson!

Intent on her thoughts as she pushed open the ornate, heavy door of the bank, she nearly collided with Charles Ladley, the mayor's son, who was just coming in.

"Why, hello, Miss Delia," he greeted her, extending a hand to steady her. "I hope everything's all right? Is there anything I can do for you?"

Delia felt a hidden amusement bubbling up within her at his concerned expression. He must think she was here to ask for a loan!

"Thank you, Charles. Everything is fine," she said serenely. "It's kind of you to ask."

He studied her more closely. "That's good, that's good. You *would* let us know if you needed anything, wouldn't you?"

Us meant the Ladleys, the pillars of the community.

"Of course I would," she said. "Tell your mother I said hello." She smiled and kept moving. It would be interesting to see how this man, on whom she had once pinned all her hopes and dreams, treated her, once he knew she was no longer the poor little church mouse.

Chapter Four

Positioned at a table by the window that faced the bank, Jude was just about to sink his fork into his savory beef stew in the Llano Crossing Hotel dining room when he spied Delia Keller exiting the bank. He straightened, seeing her almost run into the dapper man who then chivalrously kept her from falling. Jude noted, too, how the handsome swell's hand lingered a moment longer than was strictly proper on Delia's elbow.

Jude was surprised by the urge he felt to jump out of his seat and dash out the door, shouting a command for the other man to take his hands off Delia Keller. But then she smiled at her rescuer, and Jude ordered himself to remain where he was.

Obviously Delia knew the man who stared down at her so familiarly, so he needn't interfere. Delia was in no danger, and the richly dressed fellow speaking to her was perhaps the very sort of man she should be associating with from now on.

However, despite the fact that the encounter had taken no more than a minute at most, Jude couldn't quash the primitive stab of jealousy that arrowed through him as he saw Delia gift the man with a warm wave of farewell. Involuntarily his hand clenched into a fist as he watched the other man linger to eye the gentle sway of Delia's hips as she walked down the street away from the bank.

"Care for more coffee, sir?" purred a voice near his ear, and he looked up to see the waitress standing there, steaming pot in hand. She was pretty in a commonplace way, but she grinned as if they were old friends. "I'm Polly. New in town, ain't ya?" She batted darkened lashes at him and he smelled traces of a cheap floral perfume.

"Thanks," he said, deliberately ignoring her inquiry and not giving his name in return. In a small town like this she would already know that he was a stranger, anyway. He extended his cup, his gaze returning to the view out the window. Once his coffee had been refreshed, however, the waitress showed no signs of leaving.

"Who's that fancy gent standing at the bank door?" he asked, the more to keep her from asking him any further personal questions than from a real desire to know.

She put a hand above her eyes to shade them against the glare, then peered through the dusty glass, squinting. For a moment Jude thought she might actually be too nearsighted to answer him. But then she leaned down again.

"Why, that's Charles Ladley, the mayor's son," she said, sighing. "He sure is a good-looking fella. Wish he'd smile at *me* like that, though I doubt it'll do that Keller girl any good neither."

"What do you mean?" Jude kept his voice casual.

He knew it was none of his business, but he couldn't seem to keep himself from asking.

Polly gave an elaborate shrug. "Birds of a feather flock together, they say, and the Ladleys have always been as rich as King Midas. The preacher's grand-daughter—Delia Keller, that's who he was talkin' to—don't have two pennies to rub together. 'Specially now that Reverend McKinney's gone and died. Wouldn't be surprised if she don't have to come here and work 'longside a' me." There was a trace of satisfaction in her tone as she turned back to Jude.

If only you knew, Jude thought. With Delia's status about to change radically, she and the mayor's son would now be on equal footing. Any impediments to a relationship between them were about to melt like icicles in a Texas summer.

Aloud, he said, "Miss Polly, I'm sure the right man is out there, just looking for you. And when you find each other," he added, trying to sound encouraging, "he'll be so perfect for you, you'll be glad you didn't waste your time with that fellow." He kept his eyes on Ladley, who was finally entering the bank.

The waitress's eyes brightened. Jude realized that if he wanted her to go away soon and leave him to his thoughts, he'd said exactly the wrong thing.

"My, that's an awfully sweet thing for you to say, in spite a' bein' a stranger an' all that," she gushed in that suggestive voice that wasn't nearly as inviting as she apparently thought it was. She glanced quickly over her shoulder in an obvious effort to make sure the hotel owner wasn't watching, then leaned closer. "Where did you say you was from?"

"I didn't say," he said, his gaze swinging back to the window, hoping she got the hint.

But Polly was nothing if not tenacious. "You plannin' on stayin' 'round these parts? I have to work till seven, but after that I could show you around the town."

That would take all of about five minutes, he thought. "Thank you, Miss Polly, but I—"

"Or we could go to the church social next Saturday night," she interrupted. "I know about everyone in Llano Crossing, so that'd be a real nice way to meet folks.…"

He felt a twinge of pity for the girl. He hadn't even given her his name, and here she was laying out the welcome mat. He held up a hand, knowing he had to stem her flow of eagerness. "Miss Polly, much as I appreciate your kindness, I'm not sure what my plans are just yet. I'm not planning on staying long in Llano Crossing, nice as it is. I'm either going to be riding along tomorrow or doing some odd jobs for a while before I head back West."

Polly's face fell and her overbright eyes dimmed. "Sure. I understand—just wanted to be neighborly, that's all. Will you have some peach pie for dessert?"

Jude shook his head and asked her how much he owed. He would have liked some pie, but he thought it best to leave so the waitress could regain her composure. He left her an extra ten cents in addition to the dollar he owed for the meal.

Striding back into the early afternoon sunlight, Jude pondered his options. He could go to the saloon, he supposed.

In the war, he'd spent time in taverns with some of his men—too much time—between the horrendous campaigns that had led to too many lost and shattered lives. Nothing good had ever happened to him, or anyone else as far as he could see, anywhere near such a place. He'd met Nora, after all, as he was coming out of a tavern in Virginia, his judgment clouded with whiskey.

Stop thinking about her. It's over. You have to learn from it and go on.

Resist the devil, and he will flee from you, the Scriptures promised. All very well, but if he wasn't going to seek out a card game, what was he going to do with himself?

The smartest thing, he mused, would be to get his horse, Shiloh, out of the livery stable and ride west out of Llano Crossing. He could stop when he felt tired, sleep under the stars and live off the land between here and Nevada. He wouldn't have to feel responsible for watching over Delia Keller as she navigated her new life of comfort and ease. It looked like there was an even chance the mayor's son would be more than willing to take over that responsibility.

But didn't he have a moral obligation to his dead friend, Will Keller, to make sure his orphaned daughter was going to be all right, even if he wasn't going to marry Delia?

In any case, it was a waste of money to leave Llano Crossing today when he was paid through tonight at the hotel. Tomorrow he needed to have a plan, but tomorrow was soon enough. In the meantime, Shiloh was standing idle in his stall in the livery stable, no doubt eating his head off the unaccustomed rich grain and hay. Maybe the best thing to do was take the stallion on a run over the hills around Llano Crossing. They'd return in the evening, tired but content, and hopefully the silver buckskin's mile-devouring gallop would have left Jude Tucker's demons far behind.

Within fifteen minutes, Shiloh was saddled and showing his heels to the little town. For the rest of the afternoon and into the early evening, Jude and his mount explored the rolling limestone-and-cedar-studded hills, climbing until the Llano River showed as little more than a winding silver ribbon next to a collection of matchstick buildings of the town. Hawks soared overhead, taking advantage of the updrafts. Mockingbirds and crows darted among the mesquite trees and cedars, and occasionally he spied a roadrunner, darting here and there in search of the insects and snakes on which it fed.

Occasionally he spied a ranch house with outbuildings and a corral, and he knew he ought to stop and inquire if the owner needed another hand, but he felt no strong compulsion. He was enjoying the solitude and the opportunity it gave him to think.

The sun was warm on his back. He remembered, as he paused to let Shiloh drink from a cottonwood-shaded creek, how he had once used such solitary rides to gain inspiration for his sermons. It all seemed like a hundred years ago.

In those carefree days, he'd had no bigger concerns than planning next Sunday's service and wondering and praying about when the Lord was going to provide him with a wife. Every man needed a wife, but a bachelor-preacher surely had more need than most, so as to keep his concentration on the Lord's work. Fully half a dozen unmarried misses plus a widow or two decorated his front pew every Sunday morning, smiling up at him, but none of them had seemed quite right for him. Surely the Lord would shine a special light on the woman who was meant to be his wife, wouldn't He? But as yet, no such illumination had been provided.

Then the shadow of war had cast itself across the land, and Jude sensed this wasn't the time to be marrying and leaving a wife behind, her belly perhaps swelling with his child, a woman who might become a widow. The Lord was calling him to serve as one of His representatives in the army. There was time enough to think about marrying when the war was over, when—if—he resumed his position at the Mount Mulberry Church. A lot could happen during a war, he'd known, but as it turned out, he hadn't guessed the half of it.

And then the war, and the things he'd done during the war, had changed him so completely that there seemed to be no point in even trying to return to Mount Mulberry and its church. He wasn't fit to be its or anyone else's pastor anymore.

With twilight drawing on, Jude and Shiloh had descended the hills and rejoined the road back to town. Jude had been humming "Tenting Tonight," an old Civil War tune, when a shot rang out in the distance, echoing among the hills. The stallion stopped stock-still, his ears pricked forward. He gave a snort and then whinnied as if responding to a call.

Jude stopped humming, listening, too, and then he heard it—the faint cry of a man somewhere off the road among the dense mesquite and cedar. He urged his stallion off the road, navigating carefully among the cacti, the shrubs and the low trees, and after a few moments, he found the old man.

He was sitting alone on a limestone boulder, cradling his right arm, his floppy-brimmed hat shading his features.

"Howdy, stranger. I sure was thankful to hear you coming. I think this arm is broke. I tried walking, but I got to feelin' kinda fainty-like."

Jude dismounted. "What happened?" he asked, going toward the man.

"I rode out here just to have a glimpse at my old spread. Used t' live here afore me and the missus got too old t' be ranchin' anymore and moved t' town. I sold my acres to the neighboring rancher, even though I never thought much a' Dixon Miller. Anyway, I was ridin' along an' someone fired a shot—not at me, I think, but real close t' the road, like. My fool horse was so spooked, he threw me and took off," he admitted with a rueful grin. "Didn't see him run past ya, did ya?"

Jude admitted he hadn't.

"Don't know where he's got to, though it wouldn't surprise me none if Miller's boys find him and put him in with their stock. All I wanted was just a glimpse of our old home," he said wistfully, then he straightened. "James Heston's the name," the old man said, extending his other hand, though he grimaced when he loosed his careful hold on the broken right arm. His face was craggy and lined but his gaze honest and direct.

"Jude Tucker. Let me help you onto Shiloh, here, and we'll get you into town. Is there a doctor in Llano Crossing?"

The old man gave a mirthless snort. "None I'd send my worst enemy to, let alone go myself. There isn't any need, anyway. Nothing feels out of place." He felt along the forearm as if to demonstrate, wincing as he did so. "My ranch is just over that ridge. If you could just help me get home, Jude Tucker, I'll be fine. And I'm sure my missus will give you supper by way of thanks."

Jude assisted Heston to mount, thankful that Shiloh was even-tempered enough not to mind a strange rider, especially one who trembled slightly with the effort to raise his foot to the near stirrup. Then he walked alongside the buckskin in the direction of town.

They found Heston's horse halfway back. The beast had apparently cut across country and was calmly grazing. Jude mounted him rather than put Heston to the trouble of changing horses, and they rode on to Heston's house.

"That was delicious, Mrs. Heston," Jude said, two hours later, as he pushed himself back from the table and the remains of a dinner of fried chicken, black-eyed peas, corn bread and peach pie—it seemed as if he was fated to have peach pie today, even though he'd declined it at the hotel.

The comfortably plump woman with strands of iron-gray hair coming loose from her bun beamed at him. "My goodness, Mr. Tucker, it was the least I could do after you were kind enough to bring my Jim home," she said, bestowing a smile of immense warmth. "It's such a rare treat to have company, in any case."

"My wife is the best cook in these parts," James Heston bragged. He hadn't eaten that much himself, even though his wife had cut up his chicken and buttered his corn bread so that left-handed eating would be easier. His forearm was splinted now and lying in a makeshift sling of bright yellow calico, so perhaps the pain had dimmed his appetite.

She beamed. "Thank you, Jim. And what brings you to these parts, Mr. Tucker?"

"Just passin' through," he said. "I've been mining out in Nevada, but I had to come here...on some business," he said, deliberately being vague. "I'll be heading west again, soon as I raise a little traveling stake."

Heston's eyes met those of his wife. "Lookin' for work, are you?" Heston inquired.

Jude shrugged. "I might be. I've done some carpentry, but I can turn my hand to most anything."

"I'm going to need some help around here with the chores for a little while, till this bone knits itself back together. And you saw when we came in from the barn that I'm in the midst of addin' on a room to the back."

Jude nodded. Heston was about halfway through framing the addition, from the looks of things.

"We couldn't pay you much, but we'd include room and board for as long as you want to stay. It'd certainly be cheaper than the hotel or the boardinghouse."

Jude was aware that both the elderly man and his wife were holding their breath awaiting his answer. Surely their offer was an answer to a prayer he hadn't even prayed yet.

"Thank you. I'd be pleased to do that for a spell, Mr. Heston," he said, humbled by their kindness to a stranger.

Chapter Five

"**W**ho can find a virtuous woman?" Delia read in the last chapter of the book of Proverbs three mornings later after Tucker had come to see her. She loved to read her Bible there, with the sun just beginning to warm the worn wood of the rocker. Even the raucous cries of the grackles, hunting bugs among the grass, didn't usually bother her, though they could be disruptive when she tried to pray!

She was getting mighty tired of drinking her coffee without sugar, Delia mused as she sipped the unsweetened brew. She had used the very last of the sugar yesterday, so a trip back into town to sell her eggs was a must. And maybe while she was in town, Amos Dawson would see her going by the bank and run out to let her know the certificate had been confirmed by the bank in Nevada.

Delia, time enough for worldly business later. The Lord deserves your full attention right now. She could almost hear her grandfather's cracked voice saying the words.

"For her price is far above rubies." Why, it wouldn't

be long until *she* could buy rubies—or at the very least, those garnet earbobs in the window of the mercantile that she had been yearning for forever.

Oh, please, God, don't let anyone buy them before the bank in Nevada releases my money! Wouldn't it be wonderful to march right over to the mercantile and make the garnet earbobs my very first purchase?

But then in her head she heard, *"For the love of money is the root of all evil."*

The voice was so clear that she had to look around her to make sure Reverend McKinney wasn't standing behind her.

But how could it be wrong to rejoice in the windfall her father had provided for her? Her grandfather and she had had to skimp and save for so many years— surely the only thing she needed to regret was that he wasn't here to be given the comforts she could now provide!

Her eyes skipped down the page of her grandfather's well-worn Bible with his many handwritten notations in the margins to the verse: *She considereth a field, and buyeth it.*

Perhaps *she'd* be considering a field soon, though she'd rather plant a house on it than the vineyard the verse went on to mention. A big, fine, white-painted frame house, with lots of rooms. She'd have one room just to store her clothes in, another for her jewelry, an- other to entertain her many guests—perhaps even a ballroom on the second floor, with a veranda extend- ing around at least two sides of the structure.

Skimming over the verses that showed the virtuous woman rising early and working long into the night, she read, *"Her clothing is silk and purple."* Well, wasn't that marvelous? She'd love to have a lace-edged silk camisole and pantalets under a purple silk dress with a bustle. It had always been one of her favorite colors. Perhaps she would take a few minutes this very day to study the better fabrics in the mercantile, the ones she'd never even allowed herself to look at back in the hardscrabble days when she and her dear old grandfather had not been sure where supper was coming from.

But you're in mourning, a voice within reminded her, and she felt a twinge of guilt at the greedy path her thoughts had wandered onto. Propriety dictated that she wouldn't be wearing anything but black any time soon. And she would have to graduate from black slowly, lightening the somber hue with gray or lilac.

"Her husband is known in the gates," the text went on, *"when he sitteth among the elders of the land."*

"Miss Delia?" A familiar voice intruded as she read the twenty-third verse. Delia looked up to see a landau parked outside the fence and Charles Ladley coming down the stone-flagged walkway, one hand using a carved mahogany walking cane, the other clutching a bouquet of velvety red roses.

She jumped to her feet, hardly able to believe her eyes. Her abrupt motion sent the china cup clattering off the arm of the rocker. Fortunately the cup didn't break, for it had fallen into the folds of the shawl she had shed as soon as the coffee had warmed her, but it was still half-full. With dismay, Delia saw the brown liquid splash against the hem of her everyday calico dress and soak into the dark folds of the shawl.

"Oh! Charles! I—I'm sorry, I didn't s-see you coming!" she stammered, horribly aware of the untidy picture she made. Her hair was still in the plait she had

braided at bedtime last night, with tendrils escaping
it and curling wildly around her face. If only she was
wearing something better than the dress she had donned
to go feed the chickens! She had planned to change
before her trip to town. Hopefully she had no feathers
clinging to her....

"No, it's I who should apologize for intruding on a
lady in the midst of her devotions," he said with that
smile that was like a thousand lit candles. "I just came
to bring you these," he added, extending the hand that
held the roses, "picked from my mother's garden this
very morning—with her permission, of course." He
winked. As if to testify to the truth of his words, the
crimson petals sparkled with dewdrops in the sunlight.

"Thank you so much," she said, wanting to surrepti-
tiously pinch herself to make sure she wasn't dreaming.
Charles Ladley had just brought her flowers.

"Won't you have some coffee?" she said, accepting
the roses with a hand that she prayed wasn't trembling
with the delight that she felt. How heavenly it would
be to sit on the front porch sipping coffee with Charles
Ladley, for all the world to see! Wouldn't it be fun if
nosy neighbor Mrs. Purvis peeked out of her kitchen
window and saw them!

Charles's smile dimmed with regret. "I'm afraid I
can't stay—I must attend the Committee for Civic Improvement meeting that's due to start in—" he reached
down and turned the face of the gold pocket watch on
his waistcoat so he could see it "—just a few minutes.
I only came to bring you these, to let you know we
were thinking of you, Father, Mother and I, and to ask
you if you'd consent to go with me to the church social
on Saturday night. I know it's disgracefully late to be

asking you—you've probably long ago agreed to attend with some other *beau*, one of your many admirers..." His voice trailed off as if he was uncertain of her acceptance.

Delia was conscious of an urge to laugh at the very absurdity of his suggestion that she had a string of other *beaux*. "Why, no, Charles, I'm happy to say I haven't," she said, remembering not to admit no one else had asked her. "I always used to go to these occasions with Grandpa...." Her voice trailed off.

"Ah...I didn't mean to make you sad, Miss Delia," he said, leaning over to wipe away the stray tear from her eye. "If you think it's too soon since his passing to attend a social event, I'll understand." His face was a study of disappointment.

"Oh...oh no!" she said quickly, alarmed that Charles would think she was still too full of grief to be good company. "That is, I think Grandpa would *want* me to go and have a good time."

Ladley's face cleared. "Then we shall go," he said, "and lift our glasses of punch in his honor. I'll call for you at six, if that's agreeable, Miss Delia."

"That would be lovely." Then she had a sudden thought. "Charles, you know that...that is, you won't mind that I—I must wear black, will you?" She had longed forever to be invited out by Charles Ladley—now she had been and she was forced to wear that lifeless color! How she wished she could don some bright, festive color—*anything* but black! But she could imagine how tongues would wag if she violated the ironclad rules that governed mourning.

"Of course not," he responded. "Miss Delia, I've always *admired* your virtuousness, your—" he seemed to struggle for the right word "—moral excellence. I will be proud to be seen with you, even if you choose to wear a flour sack—dyed black, of course."

Delia couldn't help but chuckle with him at the thought. "I solemnly promise I will not be wearing a flour sack when you call for me on Saturday night."

He pretended to mop his brow in relief, causing her to laugh again. "Very well then," he said, bowing, as courtly as any European prince. "Six o'clock on Saturday it is."

He turned to go, and as Delia watched him walk away, she saw that he was favoring his left leg slightly, leaning more heavily on his cane when stepping onto his left foot.

"Charles, you're limping." She was touched to see him pause and turn back toward her, seemingly as loath to leave as she was to see him go. "Is your war wound bothering you?"

Everyone in Llano Crossing knew the mayor's son had marched off to join the first Texas cavalry regiment formed, and that he had been wounded and sent home in the middle of the war.

"Miss Delia, you are kindness itself to notice," Ladley said. "But don't concern yourself. Yes, the old wound aches whenever it's about to rain. With any luck it'll be better by Saturday, and I can leave this cane at home." He waved and continued down the walk to the waiting landau. Delia's heart warmed with compassion as she saw how he strove to conceal a grimace of pain as he climbed up onto the platform.

With Charles's carriage out of sight, she allowed herself a celebratory twirl of delight, hugging herself with sheer joy. Charles Ladley had asked her to the church social! He said he appreciated her virtue and her moral excellence!

Well, she might have to wear black to the church social, but it didn't have to be that borrowed, ugly bombazine she'd worn to Grandpa's funeral! She'd seen a black moire silk dress with satin ribbon trim at the neck and cuffs in the window of Miss Susan's shop, but the price tag had been one that had made her walk regretfully on. Perhaps, if she hinted to Miss Susan that she was about to come into some funds, the seamstress would extend credit to her and agree to make any needed alterations, so that Delia could go to the party, resplendent in a beautiful new dress—even if it was black!

Was it going to rain? Delia studied the sky and was surprised to see clouds forming up in the west. She must have been oblivious to them developing while she and Charles had been talking. Would she have to wait until later to do her shopping?

Absolutely not! That's what umbrellas were for! She was Miss Delia Keller, who was about to become a very rich young woman—what were mere raindrops to her? As happy as she felt, she wouldn't even notice them!

The dress fit as if Miss Susan had known she would be the one wearing it. It clung to Delia's figure, enhancing her curves without being at all revealing, and the lace trim at the waist emphasized Delia's lithe frame.

"It will only need," the rawboned, horse-faced seamstress opined, "a slight shortening of the sleeves and a few tucks in the waist, since you, Miss Delia, are one of the few ladies in Llano Crossing who don't need to be tightly corseted. It would be a joy to see my creation on you, Miss Delia."

Delia thanked her. "Would you be able to have it ready by Saturday afternoon? I would like to wear it to the church social."

"My dear, I can have it for you by tomorrow morning. Business isn't what it once was, before the war," Miss Susan said, her expression wistful.

Now came the hard part. "Miss Susan, I hate to ask this favor, but would you be able to extend me credit? Only for a week or so, I promise you," she hastened to add, as she saw dismay flash across the old seamstress's face. "I…I could leave Grandpa's watch with you as a guarantee. The truth is, while I'm not yet at liberty to discuss the details, I'm about to inherit some money."

Miss Susan eyed Delia skeptically, and Delia felt a flush of embarrassment creep up her face. Perhaps she had better resign herself to wearing the ugly, old, borrowed bombazine, after all.

"I'm afraid you'll have to give me some hint of what you mean, Miss Keller. I'm only a poor woman trying to make a living with my needle, and as I've said, that's been rather difficult in the last few years. I'd have starved to death long ago if I hadn't been wary of giving credit."

"I—I'm attending the social with Charles Ladley," Delia said, hoping to distract Miss Susan away from the source of the expected windfall.

Miss Susan's eyes brightened, and she said, "Well, that's real fine, Miss Delia. You two would make a right handsome couple, a handsome couple indeed."

Delia smothered her inward sigh of relief when the seamstress continued. "But I hope you aren't suggesting I extend you credit on the basis of one outing with the mayor's son, are you? I've lived in Llano Crossing since Charley Ladley was teething, and I've seen him squire any number of belles around. I'm sorry, but you'll have to do better than that to convince me you can eventually pay for this dress." Miss Susan held it up, brandishing it as if it were a weapon.

Delia sighed. "All right, but you must *promise* not to say a word if I tell you...." She broke off, her eyes searching the older woman's face, and seeing sympathy warring with practicality in those dark eyes behind her thick-lensed spectacles. Delia knew the moment when sympathy won—along with an honest dose of curiosity.

Miss Susan drew herself up to her full height. "I think you may safely trust in my discretion, especially toward our late preacher's granddaughter." She paused after this prim pronouncement, clearly waiting.

Delia told her the story of her father's untimely death in the mining accident and that she was only waiting to have it confirmed by the Nevada bank that her father had indeed left her a vast sum.

Miss Susan's mouth dropped open long before the end of Delia's recital, and she sank onto a nearby stool. "My, my. So *that's* where Will Keller went—I always wondered. And he left you wealthy—isn't that a wonderment?" she cried. "Why, of course you may pay me later for the dress, Delia—as long as you promise to let me continue to be your dressmaker when you come into your riches! Why, I can already picture what glorious gowns I can fashion for you, my dear! Of course, it's a pity you're in mourning, but just you wait until that time is up! I've no doubt the mayor's son will have to use that fancy cane of his to beat off your other swains, Delia!"

The two women were smiling with delight at each other when suddenly from the back came the crash of a door being shoved open with such force that it rebounded against the wall. Delia heard the intruder mutter a curse word as a muffled clatter announced that he'd knocked over something heavy.

Miss Susan gave a low cry and seemed to shrink against Delia, trembling.

"Wha—who's that?" Delia demanded, even as a cowboy, his eyes red-rimmed and bleary, shoved the curtain dividing the rooms aside and lumbered into view.

"D-Donley, y-you just wait in the back for a minute until I'm done with this customer—" Miss Susan quavered.

"Gimme it now, woman!" the man roared, lurching forward unsteadily. Even from where she stood, Delia could smell the stale whiskey fumes.

Miss Susan darted a frightened look at Delia. "Please excuse me, Miss Keller—the dress will be ready tomorrow. Now, Donley, come to the back," she said, taking hold of the drunken man's elbow and trying to guide him back in the direction from which he had come.

"I'll knock y-you inta th' middle of nesht w-week!" the man yelled, throwing Miss Susan roughly against the wall. Miss Susan screamed as Donley cocked his fist.

With a shriek of fury, Delia launched herself at the inebriated man, only to be knocked flat on her back by the man's shove. Even as she tried to right herself to go to Miss Susan's defense again, she heard a shout from outside. Then the front door was yanked open and a pair of booted legs dashed past her.

Dazed, she saw that Jude Tucker had seized Donley in a headlock and, despite the man's ineffectual attempts to hit him in the midsection while shouting slurred curse words, was silently dragging him out the door past her. Delia managed to rise just in time to see Jude throw him into the street.

He landed smack in the middle of a new pile of horse droppings. A couple of cowboys, lounging indolently across the street, straightened and strode forward as if they knew him, glaring at Jude while they hoisted the man to his unsteady feet.

"Make sure he doesn't bother these folks again," Jude told them and turned back to Delia and Miss Susan, who by now were standing at the door, open-mouthed.

He ushered them back inside. "You ladies all right?" he said, eyeing them each in turn. He gave no sign that he'd met Delia only a few days before.

Delia nodded, staring at Miss Susan, whose face was pale as bleached bones and pearled with sweat. "I'm fine. But she—he shoved her hard…"

"Why don't you sit down, ma'am," Jude said, gently propelling a shaking Miss Susan into a chair by a table stacked with dog-eared *Godey's Lady's Books*. He knelt beside the chair. "I'm Jude Tucker. I'm new in town, just staying a spell before passing on. Any bones broken?" he said, peering at her and smiling encouragingly.

Miss Susan, clearly dazed, stared at him and shook her head.

"I'm Delia Keller," Delia said, playing along. "And this is Miss Susan. It's her shop. Who was that man, Miss Susan?"

"I'm all right. Thank you, Mr. Tucker, for intervenin'. I—I'm sorry you saw that, Miss Delia. Please…"

Delia knew she was trying to find a way to ask them

to go now, to spare her any further embarrassment, but Delia knew they couldn't just leave her like that.

"Who was he?" she asked again. "I want to help you."

Miss Susan's eyes, huge behind her spectacles, blinked back tears. She buried her head in her hands.

"He won't hurt me," she said, "as long as I'm quick to give him money when he wants it."

"But why should you do that?" Jude asked. "What call does he have to demand anything of you?"

Miss Susan stared up at Delia, her lower lip quivering. "I guess the least I can do is explain after you've both come to my aid," she said. "But I depend on your discretion."

"You have it," Jude said, and Delia nodded, too.

"Donley Morrison is my husband, Miss Keller. I left him because he beat me—repeatedly."

"Your…your husband? But I thought you were never married," Delia amended hastily.

"That's what all of Llano Crossing thinks, and I prefer it that way," the older woman said, visibly gathering her dignity around her like a cloak. "I came to town believing I had eluded him, but he followed me and went to work for that rancher, Dixon Miller. Usually he leaves me alone—except when he has no money left for whiskey."

"But you've left him…" Delia stared at Jude, feeling out of her depth.

"He won't let me go. And I haven't the means to flee farther."

"I'll go get the sheriff," Jude said, rising. "He'll put him in jail for assaulting you."

"Sheriff Jenkins is one of Dixon Miller's cronies,"

Miss Susan told him wearily. "He's the wealthiest rancher in these parts."

"Then you must come and live with me," Delia said, surprising herself. "He won't bother you there."

Miss Susan shook her head. "If I don't leave things as they are, he'd force me to come back to him. He'd tell everyone he was my lawful husband and I abandoned him, and then who will come to my shop?"

"But if the truth was known—" Delia began.

Miss Susan raised a hand. "Leave things as they are. It'll be all right…though I thank you both for your kindness." She lifted her head then, her eyes pleading with them to understand her need to hang on to what pride she had left.

Delia was silent for a moment, terribly saddened by what she had just heard. "All right, Miss Susan," she said, gathering up her reticule, "but I want you to know you must come to me if anything else happens and you change your mind."

She didn't leave until the seamstress nodded.

Chapter Six

Delia was about to step up onto the boardwalk into the mercantile when Jude caught up to her.

"Are *you* all right, Miss Keller?" His cool gray-blue eyes were warm with concern. "You were on the floor when I ran in. He knocked you flat, didn't he?"

Delia smiled up at him, touched by his earnestness after his dismissive manner at the end of their first meeting. "He only hurt my pride, Mr. Tucker. It's fortunate you were passing by or things might have ended much differently. Do you think Morrison will come back to plague Miss Susan? Should I have insisted she come stay with me?" She didn't know why she expected him to know the answer to these questions.

"I'm going to go in and buy a padlock and install it on Miss Susan's back entrance," he said, with a nod toward the mercantile door. "She had a hook-and-eye latch, but there was a gap between the door and the frame wide enough for a man's hand to fit through, which I'll fix. A better lock should prevent him from surprising her from behind, least."

"Very chivalrous of you, Mr. Tucker."

He shook his head as if to say it was nothing. "And it was good of you to offer her refuge, but I don't believe she's ready yet to admit she can't handle him by herself. There may come a time, though…"

"The offer'll remain open," Delia said. His words seemed based on experience with handling people and their problems, and for a moment Delia wondered about that. But she didn't want to damage the good feeling between them, after their shared experience, by prying.

"Well, now, we've officially met, at least—though we can't exactly say how it came about," she murmured, and waited to see his reaction.

He didn't seem displeased by the idea. "That's true." But just as she hoped he'd feel free to go further with the acquaintance, he seemed to pull himself back. "I'd better not hold you up any longer. After you, Miss Keller," he said, stepping up to open the door for her.

Then they were in the midst of other shoppers in the mercantile and she didn't want to look forward by asking Jude if he'd found work and lodging, so she took her egg basket up to the counter and forced herself not to look to see what he was doing.

It was all right, Delia told herself, if Jude Tucker wasn't interested in her except as an ally in Miss Susan's defense. She was going to the church social with Charles Ladley!

Delia woke in the wee hours of the morning on the day of the church social, unsure what had roused her. Nothing seemed amiss. The only sound was the steady tick-tock of her grandfather's ormolu clock, one of the few possessions of any value that he had not sold or given away from the parlor. With the moonlight stream-

ing in her window, she could see the dark shape of the
new black dress as it hung on her wall, pressed and
ready to wear tonight at the social with Charles.

Delia tried to imagine how he would look, what they
would talk about. She must try her best to be witty and
charming, despite the fact that she had no real experience at flirting. Without letting him in on the secret of
her inheritance—for Mr. Dawson at the bank had informed her he hadn't heard anything from the Nevada
bank yet—she wanted Charles Ladley to realize she
wasn't just a timid little church mouse, the preacher's
granddaughter, anymore. Delia had seen the succes-
sion of belles on his arm just as the old seamstress had,
and she wanted to be their equal—no, she wanted to be
more enchanting than any of them!

But why had Charles Ladley come around *at this
particular time?* She froze as a sudden thought struck
her. Miss Susan had assured her of her discretion, and
so had Amos Dawson—but could she really trust the
banker as much as she did Miss Susan?

About two years ago, it had seemed for a brief time
that Charles was sweet on her, but nothing had happened; ever since then he had been nothing more than
polite. Yet three days after she had shown the bank
president the certificate from the Nevada bank, Charles
had come calling, armed with roses and an invitation.
Surely it was only a coincidence....

Her heart sank within her. Was the mayor's son co-
zying up to her now because Dawson had whispered
in his ear—or perhaps Charles's father's—that she was
about to become the richest heiress in the hill country?

Yet Charles's voice had been so courtly, his eyes so
kind and full of interest—*genuine* interest, she told

herself. He couldn't be merely putting on a show. Perhaps when Charles had failed to follow through in his flirtation with her before, it was because he had realized she was too young and too busy taking care of her grandfather. Now, with Reverend McKinney's unfortunate passing, the time was right and he was stepping forward, having never forgotten her, to show her that she was not alone in the world.

After all, he had never married, despite the numerous ladies he had courted. He had been waiting for her.

Yes, that must be it. And she could always ask him if Dawson had spoken to him about why she had come to the bank that day. If the banker had let her secret slip, Charles would either admit it, or there would be some betraying spark of guilt on his face.

There wouldn't be any such sign, though, Delia was sure of it. But she realized she was beginning to understand that wealth brought a whole new set of worries that she hadn't even had before—even before that wealth arrived.

"You do fine work, son," Heston called from his rocking chair in the shade, just as Jude pounded the last board in place that framed the new addition.

"Thank you, Mr. Heston. That's right kind of you," Jude said, taking a step back to eye his work.

"Kind, nothin'," Heston said with a snort. "Why go back to Nevada? You could probably get all the jobs you want right here in Llano Crossing." When Jude said nothing, he went on.

"You've worked real hard the past few days, Jude. Why not go along with the missus and me this evenin'?"

"Where are you going?" Jude asked, looking up.

He'd been planning on taking Shiloh out for a gallop when it cooled off, to make up for all the time the horse had had to spend in his stall while Jude worked, and he was loath to give up the plan.

"The church social. Everybody brings a special dish or two—Lucy's bringin' her fried chicken. It's quite a feast. And there's music and games, and plenty of young ladies…"

Which would mean Miss Delia Keller would surely be there. He hesitated, wanting very much to see her again, knowing he should keep to his resolution to leave her be.

"No thanks. I promised my buckskin a run at sundown."

"Aw, Jude, you got to git out among folks once in a while," Heston coaxed. "Come on, you're too young to become a hermit. Just think, there might be some young filly you'd meet there—if you went, a' course."

That was exactly what he was afraid of—only he'd already met her.

"Yes, son," Heston went on expansively, "you might meet the gal a' your dreams there at this very church social. You could build a house in town and settle down with her—"

"*Whoa,* Mr. Heston!" Jude said, holding up a hand and laughing in spite of himself. "You're getting ahead of yourself, aren't you?" In spite of his words, though, Jude felt oddly touched that the old man had called him "son." Even in the short time Jude had been staying with the old couple, they had treated him with a warmth that seemed wholly beyond what Jude felt he had any right to expect as a mere employee. But how could he explain his ambivalence about seeing Delia again? On the one hand, he knew her wealth was about to put her beyond his touch; on the other, he couldn't imagine anything he wanted more than to see her again.

"If you don't go, how'm I gonna haul that heavy basket a' food one-handed?" Mr. Heston said, pointing to his arm in a sling, with the air of one achieving checkmate.

How could he argue with that? It would be ungracious to refuse to go. It was apparently meant to be. "All right," he said with a grin. "I reckon Mrs. Heston's chicken is worth changing my plans a little."

For one wistful moment, he imagined being free to court Delia Keller without hesitation and bring her as his wife to a house he had built on the edge of town. If only there had been no fortune…

But there was no way Delia Keller, heiress to a mining fortune, could be expected to live happily ever after in what he'd be able to afford. He was a scoundrel for wishing away her good fortune, even for a moment. And he'd do well to remember that a man who had done what he had wasn't fit to court an innocent girl like Delia, even if she had not inherited a penny.

"Miss Delia, you are the very *vision* of loveliness, even in black," Charles Ladley said as she opened the door to him that evening. "I will be the envy of every man present."

Delia flushed with pleasure. The mirror had told her she looked good, but it must have understated the truth, for the light in her escort's eyes told her she was the fairest of all women.

Enjoying the elation that zinged through her at his

open admiration, she gave him a flirtatious smile. "You look very presentable yourself, Mr. Ladley."

And that was an understatement, too. His blond hair and mustache gleamed in the light shed by the setting sun. He wore a black frock coat and waistcoat over pin-striped trousers with a gleaming white shirt and string tie. A gold watch fob across his waistcoat disappeared into a pocket. A single yellow rosebud was pinned to his lapel.

"Here. My mother sent this," he said, bringing his hand, which had been hidden behind him, forward. In it was a small corsage of white roses. "She thought it would be all right if your flowers were white." He meant, she knew that it would be socially acceptable to wear white flowers with mourning.

"They're beautiful," she said. "Thank you so much, Charles." She pinned them in place on her bodice, with the pearl-headed pin that had been included, and nearly laughed out loud. How would anyone dare to openly disapprove of what she wore if she had the endorsement of the mayor's wife?

"It makes me happy to make you happy," Charles said simply.

Happy? It was all she could do not to twirl around in delight in front of him, which would surely have her escort doubting her sanity.

"Shall we go? I just need to grab my wrap," she said, reaching for the wooden peg in the hall from which hung the black *crepe lisse* shawl with the ruffled edges. Miss Susan—who had said nothing about the incident with her husband—had pressed her to take it, too, when she had come to fetch the altered dress, along with the black net gloves that she now wore. The shawl provided an elegant finishing touch to her ensemble.

Delia suppressed a shiver of pleasure as Charles took the garment from her and settled it around her shoulders, then settled her gloved hand on his arm.

Since the parsonage sat only fifty yards or so down the road from the church, they would walk. This would be her last opportunity to ask him the question. She would, of course, be reassured by his answer, and then they could have a blissful evening together—the first of many, she hoped.

"Charles," she began, having rehearsed the question—and the casualness of her tone—aloud not once, but several times, "the other day, you were just about to enter the bank—"

"Ah, you mean when I very nearly knocked you over," he said. "I'm so very sorry about that—"

She cut short his apology. "I only wondered if Mr. Dawson happened to mention why I was there."

Chapter Seven

Ladley turned eyes as limpid as a Texas creek on her and immediately answered, "Why, Delia, are you afraid Amos Dawson would gossip about your private business? I assure you, he's the soul of discretion. The man's mouth is as sealed as a tomb. I should know," he said with a rueful laugh. "I've tried to get him to loosen up about other things!"

"Sealed as a tomb" didn't seem a particularly felicitous description of the banker; nevertheless, Delia felt a lightening of her apprehension.

"So he didn't tell you—"

"The purpose of your visit? I should say not!" Then Charles grew more serious, and faced her again. "I—I assumed you had come—that is, if I may ask, were you there to ask him for a loan? Miss Delia, as we've told you before, the Ladleys would never stand for the preacher's granddaughter being in want if there was something we could do to help. And there's plenty we could do, of course. Your grandfather was always too proud to accept much of what we offered him, you know. *Was* that why you were there, Delia?"

Delia had always thought her grandfather's unwillingness to take any money for his own comforts was more a matter of humility than pride, but she was comforted by Charles's answer, and by the concern in his face.

"It's nothing you need to worry yourself with," she said, making an airy gesture as she faced forward, her voice calm but firm.

"But, Delia, the Ladleys have more than enough financial resources—"

"Charles, you must allow me to have some pride, too," she insisted, her heart singing that her misgivings about him had been for nothing.

He turned to study her as they walked along. "'Pride goeth before a fall,' Delia," he chided gently, and then, before she could give voice to her protest, made a tsk-tsking noise. "Just listen to me, having the gall to quote Scripture to the preacher's granddaughter. I'm only saying my family stands ready to help whenever you have a need. You've but to ask."

"I promise I will, if it's ever necessary," she said in a voice that she hoped made it clear that while she appreciated his kindness, the subject was closed.

He patted her gloved hand on his arm as they turned onto the flagstone path that led up to the church. "And in return for your promise, *I* promise *you* we are going to have a lovely evening, Delia Keller."

The party was being held in the yard on the east side of the church. The same long tables Jude had seen set up for the preacher's funeral dinner were laden with food once again. Paper lanterns, unlit as yet since it was still light outside, hung from ropes around the perimeter of the tables.

In the center of the tables, a fiddler was playing the bouncy tune "Wait for the Wagon."

He couldn't help but scan the crowd as he and the Hestons drew near to the church. *She might not have even come tonight,* he reminded himself, *her grandfather's death being so recent and all.* However, it was as if his eyes had a will of their own.

He saw Delia Keller the moment he stepped within the perimeter of the paper lanterns, laughing and talking to a knot of people standing around her and her escort.

It was Charles Ladley, just as he had been afraid it would be. Jude swallowed acid and fought the urge to clench his fists as he spied the proprietary way Ladley gazed down at Delia as she replied to something said to her.

"Why, there's the preacher's granddaughter," Mrs. Heston cooed. "Doesn't she look pretty, in spite a' all that's happened to her lately? Even dressed in black. And isn't that the mayor's son standin' next to her? My, my, when did that happen? No wonder she's lookin' a little less melancholy than she did before!"

"When did *what* happen?" Heston growled beside her. "Ain't no law against someone standin' next to someone, last I heard. That don't mean they came together!"

"But I was planning to introduce Miss Delia to Jude," Mrs. Heston said, her tone disappointed. "Seemed to me she'd be perfect for our Jude."

"Why, so she would," agreed Mr. Heston. "Introduce 'em anyway. You never know what might happen."

Our Jude? He wondered when he had become that. As much as he cherished the old couple's warmth, he had to put a stop to their matchmaking.

He held back. "Mrs. Heston, I've told you I'm not planning on staying in town long—" he began, but Lucy Heston ignored him like the force of nature she was.

"Now, don't be bashful, Jude. A little acquaintance-makin' never hurt anybody," she said. "Oh, Delia!" she called, moving faster than Jude had known the plump woman could.

There was no avoiding the meeting. Already Delia was watching Mrs. Heston approach, though she had apparently not caught sight of Jude yet, bringing up the rear with Mr. Heston.

"Hello, Mr. and Mrs. Heston. Mr. Heston, whatever happened to you?" she asked, nodding toward his sling.

"Horse threw me." He turned toward Jude, but before he could make the introduction, his wife spoke up. "Delia, how are you gettin' along, dear?" She took Delia's two hands in her own and stood on her tiptoes to kiss the girl's cheek. "I declare, you have never looked better! And, Charles Ladley, how are you?"

She barely listened to the man's murmured answer before her attention swung back to Delia.

"Delia Keller, we'd like to present our new friend, Jude Tucker. He happened along when Jim was thrown and he's been a godsend, helping out around our place."

"Actually, we've already met, Mrs. Heston," Delia said, darting a look at him before going on to say, "Mr. Tucker happened to be installing a lock at Miss Susan's shop the same day I went in for this dress."

It was a neatly formed answer—not a lie, but not the

full truth, either, so as to protect Miss Susan's reputation. He sent her an approving look.

A sudden hectic color flooded her cheeks. "Nice to see you again, Mr. Tucker," she said, extending her gloved hand. "Are you planning to stay long in these parts?"

He shrugged as his eyes drank in her appearance. "I don't rightly know just yet, ma'am. I've come from out West—" *as you know* "—and I might only be staying long enough to earn a stake to travel back there."

"But if we could give him some reason, Delia dear, maybe we could talk him into staying...." Mrs. Heston let the heavy-handed hint dangle in the air.

As if he was determined not to be ignored any longer, Charles Ladley spoke up. "Why, the lovely town and its generous people are reason enough, wouldn't you say, Mrs. Heston? Charles Ladley," he said, extending a hand to Jude. "The mayor's my father. If we can be of any assistance to you..."

Ladley's voice trailed off as he shook Jude's hand. His nails were manicured and looked as if dirt had never clung to them, but they weren't the smooth hands of a man who had never done any manual labor. Jude spotted the way Ladley leaned on his cane without obviously depending on it and the tightness of his mouth; he knew Ladley was acquainted with pain. Perhaps he'd misjudged the man. Ladley had seen army service, unless Jude missed his guess.

Ladley bent low and murmured into Delia's ear, "Father's beckoning us. I think dinner's about to begin." He straightened and faced Jude and the Hestons. "If you'll excuse us..." He swept Delia past them.

"Never you mind, Jude," Mrs. Heston said, patting

his shoulder as if he needed consolation. "I have a notion this is only the first time they've been out together, so nothing's set in stone between those two. You still have a chance."

Jude was wondering what he could say to that when the older man spoke up. "Now, Mrs. Heston, there are plenty of other fish in the sea for a handsome fella like Jude. And he can handle those matters himself. We ought t' butt out."

"Nonsense. I think they'd be perfect for one another," Mrs. Heston argued, but at that moment the mayor announced that all was ready. He would say the blessing, and then everyone should line up at the serving table, mothers and small children first.

His prayer was as practiced a piece of oratory as Jude had ever heard and went on long enough that Jude could hear little boys and girls growing restless among the crowd. The mayor extolled the beauty the Lord had bestowed upon the river and the hills around them and the twilight sky above. "Bless those who mourn among us, most notably our own Delia Keller, who has been so recently bereaved...."

Jude was sure that he would have mentioned each townsperson separately if a baby had not begun to wail.

"And thank you for the bounty laid before us of which we are about to partake, amen," he finished hastily.

"*Humph.* I heard the mayor's going to do the Sunday sermons at church until they get a new preacher," Mrs. Heston remarked, and it did not appear to Jude that the prospect made her happy.

"Wordy, pompous old coot," muttered her husband, as he urged his wife forward into the line.

As Heston had indicated, there were a handful of other young ladies present of varying description, and most of them found an excuse to come chat with the Hestons at their table. Mrs. Heston was in her element, introducing Jude.

Jude, standing as he was presented, was pleasant to each one and made conversation for as long as the girl lingered, but after they'd all gone back to their seats, he'd seen none of them that was Delia's equal.

"Maybe you kin eat your chocolate cake in peace if you hurry," Heston said with a chuckle. "But watch out, boy. You're a marked man now, right enough. You'll see that when you come to town, and I wouldn't be surprised if we began gettin' more visitors at the house than usual."

"It's the war," Mrs. Heston explained. "These girls hardly ever see a new fellow in town. Even two years later, it seems all that's left 'round here is graybeards and men who've come back minus a leg or an arm—not that they're not worthy, of course."

Jude pretended to listen, just as he'd pretended to enjoy each introduction. It had been nearly impossible not to look past each girl to where Delia was sitting with Ladley and his parents.

She was only picking at her food, but that didn't seem to distress her. On the contrary, she appeared to be having the time of her life, laughing at Ladley's remarks and chattering away, her graceful, long-fingered hands gesturing as she spoke. Once or twice she leaned past Ladley to answer something Mr. or Mrs. Ladley had asked, and Jude had seen Charles gaze fondly at her bent head.

The sound of a man clearing his throat at the head

table where Delia was sitting barely penetrated Jude's consciousness, but then he saw Delia turn her head to look at the older man getting to his feet down the table from him.

"I'd like to make an announcement," the paunchy, well-dressed man said and waited as all around him, the people of Llano Crossing, put down forks and glasses and lifted their heads.

"That's Amos Dawson, th' banker," Heston whispered. "Wonder what he's gonna say. Hasn't the mayor done enough speechifyin' for one evenin'?"

"Now you hush, James Heston, or we won't be able to hear," his wife hissed.

"Our gracious mayor has alluded earlier to those who mourn among us, specifically our own Miss Keller," the banker began.

Jude saw Delia's eyes grow wide and the color drain from her face. Her jaw dropped open as if she wanted to speak. Jude realized at once that she knew what Dawson was about to say and that if she could have stopped him, she would have. But the man only smiled beneficently as she made a move as if to stand, and he gestured for her to remain seated.

"Now, Miss Delia, let me speak. You've always been the very essence of humility, not wanting any attention for yourself," he said. "But there are people who have been worried for you, and now you must allow them to share in your joy at the news I am about to bring."

"No, please, I don't think—" Jude heard her say. All at once Jude also knew what the banker was about to announce and why Delia wanted so desperately to keep him from speaking.

"The longtime residents of this town will remember

that many years ago Miss Delia's father, Will Keller, rode off to seek his fortune out West after the tragic loss of his wife, Miss Delia's mother. When time passed and he did not return, most of us thought something ill had befallen the man and that Delia would likely never see her papa again, alas." Dawson paused to look over the crowd, avoiding Delia's pleading gaze. Satisfied that every eye was trained on him, he opened his mouth again. "But recently Miss Delia received some news that is bittersweet. Sadly, it is true that her father is dead, but he died only recently. In dying, however— and this is the sweet part, folks—he has left her the sole heiress to a fortune in silver mining profits."

Chapter Eight

Delia's cry of horror at the news being blurted out was drowned in the collective gasp of the crowd.

Succeeding at last in rising on legs that shook as if she was standing on stilts, she stared at Dawson, stammering, "You...you had no r-right..." But her words were smothered in the thunder of applause and cheers from the townspeople around her.

Dawson ducked his eyes, making motions with his hands to encourage the crowd to keep clapping and cheering.

Charles had risen, too, and had an arm around her shoulders. "Delia, dear, what an amazing thing! That is to say, I'm so sorry to hear about your father's passing, of course, but how wonderful he has left you this legacy!" His surprise seemed real enough.

"But, Charles, Mr. Dawson shouldn't have—"

He made a tsk-tsking noise. "Such news was bound to leak out soon enough," he said into her ear as he squeezed her shoulder bracingly. "And rumors would have been flying if folks had learned the news by word of mouth—you know how facts get distorted that way."

"My son's right," chimed in Mayor Ladley. "You would have been plagued with everyone's curious questions as to whether it was true. This way, everyone has heard the truth at once."

"Dear, you must allow them to rejoice with you," Jane Ladley urged. "They all wish you well."

Cries of "Speech! Speech!" and "Miss Delia, what're you going to do with all that money?" rose from the rows of tables, aimed right at her, like small stones. Every eye was on her, each person holding his or her breath to hear what she would say.

Delia opened her mouth to speak. "I...I..." She faltered. "This...all this is so n-new to me. I've hardly had time to take it in...especially since it comes with...very sad news. I hope you'll all believe me when I say I'd rather have my father back than one penny of this inheritance." She shrugged, not knowing what else to say.

As the crowd applauded again, their faces sympathetic, Delia turned to her escort, imploring, "Charles, please, would you take me home?"

"Of course, sweetheart," he murmured.

A respectful silence fell over the crowd as Delia settled her shawl around her shoulders, and Charles held out his arm to her.

"I'm sorry, Miss Delia," Dawson said, stepping forward as if to intercept her. "I meant no disrespect to the dead, you understand. I just thought everyone would want to celebrate with you."

"We will speak later, Mr. Dawson," Delia said, keeping her tone level but quickening her steps as she passed by the banker. This wasn't the appropriate setting to discuss such a matter, and she was so angry with the banker that she couldn't have trusted herself to talk with him anyway.

So angry that she had forgotten that Jude Tucker was sitting somewhere in the crowd and had seen the whole embarrassing fiasco unfold—until her eyes met his as she approached where he and the Hestons had been sitting.

He stood as she drew near and gave her a barely perceptible nod. The look in his pale eyes was one of rueful sympathy, as if he understood her dismay even better than she did. Delia felt at that moment that he comprehended her feelings perfectly.

Hardly realizing she was doing it, Delia straightened her spine and lifted her head as they left the churchyard.

Charles was silent for the short time it took them to walk down the moonlit road to her house. Then, as they reached her gate, he cleared his throat.

"Delia, I understand that you are mourning a tragic loss. Why, I can't even comprehend losing a parent...."

Delia turned her chin to look at him, but in the shadows, Charles's face was guileless.

"But I hope you will forgive me if I ask you a question." He waited until she had nodded her assent before speaking. "Don't you think your father would want you to be happy and enjoy your good fortune, not feel guilty that you're receiving it because he is no longer with you?"

She seized upon the euphemism in his question. "My father hasn't been 'with me,' as you put it, for a good part of my life. Why should I feel guilty?"

He studied her for a moment. "A poor choice of words, sweet Delia, but you know what I meant." He had stopped outside her gate and stood to face her, leaning his cane against the low stone wall.

"You meant he is *dead*," Delia said with deliberate emphasis. "I don't know why everyone is too careful to say that word around me." She was astonished at the bitterness that had flown out of her and wished she hadn't spoken so to Charles, of all people. What must he think of her now?

"I'm so sorry, Charles, I can't imagine what made me speak so sharply...." Delia began, but then tears drowned the rest of her apology.

Suddenly Charles was pulling her into the circle of his arms. She felt safe as the storm of her emotions broke across her.

"My poor dear, you've had such a difficult time," he murmured, his voice and his touch soothing. He let her cry for a few minutes, then he lifted his head as if hearing something from the direction of the church.

"Perhaps we should step inside your parlor, Delia dear," Charles said. "It sounds as if the party is breaking up, and—"

She didn't want the good folk of Llano Crossing to pass by on the way to their homes and see her weeping on Charles Ladley's shirtfront.

"I suppose you're right," she said, and led the way up the porch and into the house. She felt a little strange about what she was doing—she had never been alone with a man before, except for her grandfather or Amos Dawson at the bank, if that counted.

Once inside, however, she strove to calm herself by lighting the lamp on the table. When its soft glow filled the room, she turned back to Charles. "Please, sit down," she said, pointing to a threadbare horsehair couch while she sank onto the ladder-back chair nearby. "May I offer you a glass of tea?"

He waved away her offer. "No, thank you, Delia, but I'm as full as a tick that just fell off an old hound's back, as my colonel used to say back in the war."

The folksy way of speaking made her smile, as he must have known it would, since it wasn't his usual correct style of speaking. Then Delia saw a pensive expression cross his face. Of course—he had suffered in the war, and had returned with chronic pain and a cane.

"I won't stay long," he said. "It wouldn't be proper, I'm well aware. I just wanted to say that I think I know why you're distressed at what that fool Amos Dawson said."

"You do?"

He nodded. "Delia, you're used to being a very private person, and now everyone knows your business. That is the lot of the wealthy, you know," he informed her. "Everyone knows, or thinks they know, everything about you. I've experienced it since I was just a boy, Delia, and despite the Yankees' attempts to ruin the South's gracious way of living, the Ladleys still enjoy a comfortable life. But you've had that change thrust on you without warning, and you feel a bit…*uncovered,* if I may be forgiven for such an indelicate description. Isn't that right?"

She blinked in surprise. Yes, that was *exactly* how she felt. How wise, how understanding Charles was! Surely he had been sent by God to help her.

As if he could read her thoughts, Charles smiled and cupped her cheek in a caressing hand. "Don't you worry, Delia Keller. You're not alone any more, struggling to find your way. I hope we're going to see a lot more of each other, for I'd like to be there every step of the way to help you in your new life."

"You're so kind," she said. Hadn't this been what she'd dreamed of all along, having Charles at her side? Only now there would be no inequity of social position between them. It was too perfect!

"I'd best be on my way," he said, picking up his cane. "But before I go, I have something for you to think about, Delia."

Was he going to invite her out again? Where would he suggest going? "And what's that, Charles?" she asked, smiling up at him. She could hardly wait to hear what his question would be.

"What's the very first thing you would like to do with your money?"

His question was so far from what she had been thinking he would say that for a moment she was disappointed. But she wanted him to admire her for having a businesslike approach to her wealth, so she forced herself to refocus her thoughts.

"I would like to buy land and build a house," Delia told him. "A fine house, one of the best in Llano Crossing. I have to admit I'm tired of living with a leaky roof in a tiny building that lets in all the cold in the winter and all the heat in the summer."

Charles laughed. "That's the spirit! Nothing's too good for you, Delia Keller. You've been a poor little church mouse long enough."

His approval washed over her like a balm. So why did she hear the voice of her grandfather in her heart, asking what she was going to do for the Lord with her money?

But Charles was speaking again, and his voice

drowned out her grandfather's. "But, Delia, why don't you wait awhile and see what the future has in store for you? Why, some handsome prince is apt to happen along, complete with his own castle, and sweep you off your feet. Then you would have spent a large chunk of your money for nothing." A small smile played about Charles's perfectly formed lips.

Delia stared at him. Was his high-flown way of speaking a way of hinting *he* wanted to be her prince?

She felt suddenly more sure of herself and decided to test Charles a bit.

"Why, who says I'll even *want* a husband, Charles Ladley? If I'm to be a woman of means, perhaps I won't even need someone to rule over me and tell me what I may spend my money on."

He seemed amused by her assertion. "No wise man would ever dream of doing so, Miss Delia. He would just count himself lucky he could share your life. And now good night, my dear."

Holding both her hands between his, he allowed himself a sigh of regret as he headed for the door. "Until we meet again…"

"Gonna get some shut-eye, Jude?" Mr. Heston asked, after they returned to their little house in town. Jude had just turned toward the barn. Although the Hestons had offered him their spare room, he'd fixed up a pallet in the small barn's tackroom and that suited him just fine.

Jude shook his head. "I reckon I'm too wide-awake to sleep just yet. I think I'll give Shiloh that gallop I promised him earlier. We'll be quiet when we return, I promise."

Heston considered that, looking out the window to

peer at the full moon. "I s'pose it *is* pert' near bright as day out there, ain't it?" He turned back to Jude. "Goin' t' ride by the parsonage, to see if Miss Delia's light's still on?"

Jude paused, with one hand on the back door, then forced himself to reply casually. "No, why would I do that?"

"I got eyes in my head, son," came the old rancher's quick reply. "I saw how you were lookin' at her."

Jude sighed. He was going to have to find some polite way to deter Heston from reading his mind.

"I told you, Mr. Heston—"

"Why don't we stop the 'Mr. Heston' stuff and call me Jim? We're friends, ain't we?"

"All right, then—Jim, I told you I don't intend to court any ladies here," Jude said evenly. "I took this job so I could raise a stake to go back out West."

Now it was Heston's turn to sigh. "I'm sorry, Jude. Lucy tells me I need to learn t' tend my own knittin', and that's a fact. Forgive a curious old man, won't you? But there was somethin' about the way you were watchin' her...and watchin' Ladley watchin' her," he added frankly. "Just thought you might be goin' to see if Ladley had left her house yet. Yeah, I spied him goin' into the house with her as we left the social, same as you did," he said when Jude peered more closely at him. "And for what it's worth, I think you'd be a darn sight better man for her than the mayor's boy."

"He's hardly a boy," Jude countered. "He's been a soldier, after all."

"Aw, I remember when that pup was knee-high to a bumblebee," Heston retorted. "But what about you and Delia?"

"You heard the same news about her that I did tonight."

"That she's livin' in tall cotton now? Yeah, so what?"

"So I've got as much in common with the young lady now as I have with that moon up there," he said, nodding toward the sky. "She'll have enough fortune hunters beating a path to her door without me getting in line."

"You ain't no fortune hunter," Heston insisted, his chin jutting out stubbornly. "You were lookin' at her that way afore the announcement was ever made. I'll shut my mouth now an' let you get on with your ride. See you in the mornin'."

Jude made short work of saddling Shiloh. Minutes later, he was galloping up the road on the stallion's back, savoring the smooth play of the powerful beast's muscles beneath him and the sight of the horse's moonlit shadow eating up the ground beside him.

He deliberately rode away from town for a while, as if to deny even to himself that Heston's guess had been right about his destination. But a couple of miles up the road from where he'd first encountered the old man, the road began to climb steadily upward. Jude was too good a horseman to tax his mount by running him uphill, so he reined Shiloh around, slowed the stallion to a lope and headed back to Llano Crossing.

Most of the buildings in the town were dark, though the saloon was doing a roaring business, to judge by the tinkly music of the piano and the bright lights spilling from its dusty windows and over the batwing doors.

He might as well go ahead and do what he had really come for. Jude slowed the stallion to a trot in the direction of the far side of town and Delia Keller's house.

He hadn't realized he was holding his breath until he rounded the bend in the road. The shadowy outline of the old preacher's former abode appeared as a rectangular mass under the oak trees that blocked much of the moon's brilliance. Not one tiny candleflame shone through the drawn calico curtains at the windows.

So Delia had gone to bed, Jude thought, relieved.

"Love bears all things, believes all things, hopes all things, endures all things," a Voice suddenly reminded him, and he realized that this was the Voice he should have been listening to all along.

He smiled ruefully as he continued to gaze at the house. *Love?* Why on earth would that verse have occurred to him? On what crazy basis could he say he *loved* Delia Keller? He hardly knew her—or she, him. He had just been a messenger to her, a bearer of mixed tidings at best. His role in her life was already over, no matter how pleased she had seemed to be tonight when she saw him.

But there it was, as sure as the moon hung over his head. He loved her. *Lord, what can you be thinking?*

My ways are not your ways, the still small Voice reminded him.

He studied the house again. There was a quietness, a peace to it that somehow didn't seem possible if two people had been inside it, awake and doing things he wouldn't allow himself to think about.

Jude sighed. It was time to get home and get some rest, even if he couldn't sleep—

"Jude, is that you?" a voice said from deep in the shadows of the porch.

Chapter Nine

Jude almost fell off his horse in astonishment as a small, shawl-swathed figure detached itself from the rocker and took a step or two forward.

"Delia?" he said, hardly sure if it was really her or just wishful thinking on his part. He was barely aware of dismounting and going toward her. "What are you doing, sitting out here in the dark?" As he drew closer, he could see her more clearly. She wore some sort of flower-sprigged everyday wrapper in place of the elegant black dress he'd seen her in earlier. Bare feet peeped out appealingly from beneath the wrapper's hem. Her hair had been taken down and hung in luxurious curls nearly to her waist. He longed to touch it.

He noticed also that she had dropped the formality of calling him "Mr. Tucker," nor objected when he called her by her first name, too.

"I could ask you the same thing," Delia retorted. "At least I'm not out riding around in the dark."

"Dark? It's pert' near bright as day," he said, smiling as he quoted the old rancher. "Couldn't you sleep?"

Delia shook her head.

He could hardly believe that Delia wasn't already beating a hasty retreat inside her door. Her neighbors wouldn't think it proper for them to be visiting like this.

He took a step closer. "Are you still upset about the banker spouting your news like he did?"

Her gusty sigh stirred the ruffle along her neckline. "Yes," she admitted. "I suppose in the end it'll be easier than having to tell all the details over and over again, but I wish Mr. Dawson had asked me first." She sank down on the top step, and amazingly, patted the area next to her, clearly inviting him to sit.

Jude did as she bid, but he was careful not to sit too close.

"Charles thinks I'll have a lot to get used to now that my situation has changed," Delia said, not looking at him.

He hated having to agree with anything Ladley said, but he could hardly disagree. "He's right. Everything will be different now," he said carefully, wondering where this was leading.

Her face was lovely in moonlit profile. "I want to buy a house," she said, surprising him yet again. "A large house. A really nice house. Do you think that's silly?"

He didn't know why she was asking, but the answer seemed very important to her.

"No," he said, choosing his words carefully. "You can hardly go on living here forever—"

"That's what I was thinking," she broke in in a rush. "The church will call a new pastor, sooner or later, and I'll need a new place to live. I…" Her voice trailed off as if she would've said more but didn't think it wise.

"If you're asking me, I—I think you should pray about it, and ask God to find you the right place. But then go ahead. You've got a lot of money, Delia. Your father wanted you to be able to live well."

His answer seemed to please her, and she smiled tremulously at him. "Yes, it seems he did, didn't he? You don't...that is, you don't think I should wait until I am married to have a house, do you?"

He tried to hide his amazement that she was asking him this question. "I think," he said, praying that the Lord would give him the right words, "that the same God who would find you the right house will be able to arrange all other aspects of your life for the best."

"Thank you, Jude," she said, eyes lit with appreciation. "How did you get to be so wise?" Impulsively, she leaned forward and kissed him on the cheek.

He was still for a few seconds, absorbing the fact that Delia Keller had just kissed him, and then he let his lips turn toward hers, his heart singing with joy. He lowered his head...

The snapping of a twig outside the gate seemed as loud as the crack of a gunshot, startling them away from each other. Jude was on his feet in a flash, the wariness of the war years causing him to instinctively shield Delia from whoever had been trying to sneak up on them.

"Who is it? Who's there?" he called, reaching for a pistol he no longer wore.

"It—it's only me," called a quavery female voice from the road. "I'm sorry...sorry to intrude."

Delia recognized her first. "Miss Susan?" she cried, leaping to her feet and running down the walk to the woman who stood outside her gate in a patch of silvery moonlight.

She was inches from the woman when the ethereal

glow illumined the woman's disheveled hair, the scrape on one cheek, the swollen-shut eye and the ragged tear in her sleeve. At her feet lay a worn, stuffed carpetbag.

"Miss Susan, what happened to you?"

"I...I waited as l-long as I could...." the woman stammered, still hesitating. "I d-didn't want anyone to see me...wanted to make s-sure *he* didn't see me... I'm sorry to intrude," she said again, looking from Delia to Jude and back again.

"Don't give it a thought," Jude said, coming forward to join Delia now and usher the woman into the house. "Did your husband do this?"

Shoulders sagging, Miss Susan nodded and let them help her inside. "He was all liquored up. He didn't really even know what he was doing."

"When did he do this?" Delia asked grimly, settling Miss Susan into a chair in the parlor.

The woman nodded. "I...I was late leaving the shop, and he caught me between it and my room at the boardinghouse. Mrs. Mannheim thought...that is, she helped me pack and said perhaps I'd better take you up on your promise to take me in."

"Of course you must stay here with me," Delia said, kneeling by Miss Susan and stroking her arm. Her eyes met Jude's.

"And tomorrow morning I'll go with you to make a complaint at the sheriff's office," Jude said.

"Nooooo!" moaned the woman.

Jude was firm. "He has to know that decent people won't allow him to treat you that way, Miss Susan—"

"But tomorrow is Sunday," she pointed out. "Everyone will be passing through town on the way to church. I can't stand for them to see me like this!"

Delia's face was sympathetic. "You know, I'd for-gotten tomorrow was Sunday," she admitted. "Sheriff Jenkins will be at church. I'll ask him to call on us here in the afternoon."

"If you need me to confirm what happened at the shop, just have him call on me at the Hestons'," Jude said.

Assured that Delia could help the woman bathe her scrapes and bruises and would make her comfortable in her spare bedroom, Jude took his leave a few min-utes later. He'd had a feeling that Miss Susan's abuser would strike again, but even he hadn't thought it would be this soon. He hoped that Delia's taking the woman in wouldn't expose her to danger, too. And they'd have to be sure, Jude decided as he remounted his buckskin and headed back toward town, that one of them was available to escort the seamstress to and from her shop.

The saloon was still full of noisy drinkers, though the piano player had evidently taken a break, because no music drifted toward Jude as he neared the estab-lishment. But as Jude drew abreast of the far side of the building, where a stairway on the side of the build-ing led up to the second floor, he heard the sound of a footfall at the top.

During his time in the army, an unexpected sound might have meant a sniper was taking position to fire. Jude halted Shiloh in the shadow of the saloon and peered upward.

He saw Charles Ladley outlined in the moonlight at the top of the stairs, holding the door open, and heard a woman's voice. Then a bare arm reached out, hand-ing Ladley his silver-headed cane.

Jude prayed Ladley wouldn't see him—and that the

stallion didn't betray Jude's presence by snorting or stamping.

The two at the top of the stairs shared a chuckle.

"Thanks, honey, I'd have forgotten that," Ladley murmured and leaned back into the doorway a moment. Then, grinning, he resumed his descent and disappeared into the far alleyway behind the building.

Jude was thoughtful about what he had just seen, well aware that the upper floor of the saloon was where the saloon girls took the customers who wanted to spend private time with them, so to speak.

The impulsive kiss Delia had bestowed upon Jude's cheek may have only been meant in a friendly way—he didn't know, for Miss Susan's arrival had interrupted him just as he was about to kiss her in return. He didn't know how she truly felt about Charles Ladley.

What if she was smitten with Ladley? Jude was sure she didn't know the man secretly liked spending time with women of ill repute. Did Jude have an obligation to tell Delia what he had seen?

He listened for the still small Voice, but at the moment it was silent.

Even if it hadn't meant leaving Miss Susan alone at the house, Delia would have dreaded going to church. It had always been the highlight of her week before. Now, however, not only was her beloved grandfather gone, but there would be no preacher in the pulpit. Also, last night's revelation of her new fortune would still be uppermost in the minds of many of the townspeople. She would have to face their questions after the service.

But Charles will be there, she reminded herself,

humming a hymn as she dressed. She'd have to find a time to tell him about Miss Susan staying with her.

What about Jude Tucker? Would he attend? Last night, he hadn't mentioned going. What had he thought of her kiss? She was almost certain he had been about to kiss her—and not only on her cheek as she had done, either—but then Miss Susan had arrived and the moment had ended.

Charles was waiting for her at the church door. He led her to the front pew where his mother was sitting. His father was already standing by the pulpit. Jane Ladley was all graciousness in her greeting as Delia took her place between her and Charles. Delia, who had always used the time before the opening hymn to quiet her heart and turn her mind toward worship, hoped she wasn't expected to make lively conversation with the mayor's wife.

She was in luck. She had no sooner settled herself when Mrs. Purvis struck up the first notes of "Shall We Gather at the River" on the aged organ. Those already seated stood and began to sing while stragglers filed in.

During the second hymn, Delia spotted the Hestons in one of the middle pews. Jude Tucker, however, was not among them.

So he isn't a churchgoer. It's none of your concern, anyway, she told herself, wrenching her attention back to the words of the song and Charles's pleasant tenor.

Charles Ladley Sr. read one of the Psalms and then expounded on it in a resonant, formal voice. Fortunately he kept his remarks brief, ending modestly with a hope that a new pastor would soon be obtained to replace him so he could return to "merely" being the mayor. Everyone smiled in sympathy and a few chuckled.

Afterward, Delia found the presence of the Ladleys as good as a fence. She was greeted, but no one aimed any inquisitive remarks her way. She took advantage of the Ladleys' being drawn into conversation with Barton Jeffers, the mill owner, to ask Sheriff Jenkins to come speak to Miss Susan that afternoon, and he rather grudgingly agreed.

"Delia, dear, will you join us for dinner at our home this afternoon?" Mrs. Ladley asked her when she rejoined them.

Delia regretted having to explain why she must decline the gracious invitation. "It's so nice of you to ask, but Miss Susan is staying with me for a few days, and I don't want to leave her alone."

She saw Charles raise an eyebrow. "Oh? When did this come about?" he asked. She knew he was thinking that he'd seen no sign of her the night before when he'd come inside.

"Why not bring her along? The more the merrier!" boomed the mayor, standing behind his son.

Delia cleared her throat. "She…ah…I'm afraid she isn't feeling very well right now. Perhaps another time." She was aware of Charles's curious gaze, but she didn't want to explain more fully in front of his parents.

Delia was pensive as she prepared to leave the house the next morning. Prior to the church social and its aftermath, she had thought she might go into town Monday morning, stopping at the bank to make her first withdrawal from her account—not a large amount, but enough to pay for what she wanted. She'd then stop at Miss Susan's, where she would commission some more dresses, as well as several camisoles and petticoats of the softest lawn and the finest lace trim the seamstress could lay her hands on.

Then she would go to the general store and buy some provisions. This time she wouldn't have to limit herself to only necessities, such as flour and sugar and cornmeal. Why, if she chose, she could buy fancy jellies some *other* woman had put up or a whole sackful of peppermint sticks. And if Mr. Dean still had that lovely paisley shawl in his window, the one with the long, silky black fringe, why, it wouldn't be hanging there any longer than it took for her to snap it up.

It would be so much fun, she'd been thinking, being able to do as she wanted, rather than having to hoard every cent and pester her hens for eggs to sell. She stared in the cracked mirror in her room and thought it would be nice to buy a new mirror, one that reflected faithfully the elegant lady she was becoming. Perhaps she could find some scented cream there, too, to rub into her dry, work-worn hands, so that they became smooth like those of a woman of means, who had other people scrub her floors and wash her dishes.

Miss Susan's presence had changed her carefree mood. The seamstress had announced this morning that she wasn't going to her shop until the swelling and bruising went down around her eye, and she asked Delia to insert a note on the door that the shop was closed until further notice. Despite the sheriff's gruff assurance that he would order Donley Morrison to leave his wife alone, Delia could understand the woman's reluctance to face the curious and pitying glances of the townspeople. It would take a week, at least, before the bruising faded. How much ought she to encourage

Miss Susan to trust the townspeople's compassion and return to her regular routine?

Just as Delia inserted her final hairpin, a knock sounded at the door. Who could be calling so early? Peeking out the bedroom window, she saw that it was Jude Tucker.

She assumed he had come to check on Miss Susan, but, still, his unexpected appearance had her flying to the door as if her feet had wings.

"Good morning, Jude. My, you're up bright and early today," she said, beckoning for him to enter. "Would you like some coffee? Have you had your breakfast? We've eaten, but I could scramble some eggs, and I believe there's some jam left."

"And good morning to you, Delia," he said. "Don't you look pretty this morning? No thank you. Mrs. Heston already made her husband and me a huge breakfast."

"Are you here to check on Miss Susan?" she said, lowering her voice. "She's in the other room dressing, but I'm sure she'll be out in a minute—"

"She's doing all right? Jenkins came and listened to her account?"

"He did," she said. "And he swears he'll make sure Miss Susan won't have to worry about Morrison bothering her again. But she's still not feeling up to going to work."

"I'd give her a few days," Jude said, his eyes thoughtful. "And yes, I came to see about her, but also I'd like to take you to see something."

She stared at him. "What? Where?"

He grinned. "It's a surprise," he said. "You'll see when you get there."

Chapter Ten

"You're not going to tell me before we get there?" Delia asked as they left her house. He'd borrowed the Hestons' buckboard, she noticed.

His eyes danced teasingly as he settled himself on the seat next to her. "No, ma'am. That's why it's called a surprise."

Jude directed the horse west down the dusty road. "You haven't been out this way lately, have you?"

She shook her head. "I've been pretty much a homebody since Grandpa got so frail. Everything we needed was in town."

The buckboard rolled on for a couple of miles until it came to a bend in the road, and then Jude pulled to a halt and said, "Now close your eyes, please, to get the full effect."

Obediently, Delia complied. She felt the wagon roll go around the turn in the road, and then Jude called, "Whoa."

"Now you can open your eyes," he said beside her.

There before her, on a gentle rise above the Llano River, sat the wooden frame of a large, unfinished two-story house. It was flanked by cottonwoods and a barn, with a couple of venerable, gnarled oak trees shading the front.

Delia blinked. "Whose place is this?"

Jude's smile broadened. "Yours, if you choose to make it so, Delia. It includes five acres, too."

She continued to stare at him in confusion. "But who started this? Why didn't they finish it?"

"I'm told a couple of Yankee speculators bought the site from an old couple—did you know the Delaceys, who moved to Houston? The speculators razed the smaller old house and started to build."

Delia searched her memory. "I remember the Delaceys moving. They were two of the oldest members of the church. And I heard about two Yankees coming to town, trying to buy up land right after the war, but I never heard what became of their project. Grandpa didn't keep up with such things. Do you know what happened to them?"

"Mr. Heston said some men in the town convinced them they wouldn't be happy here after all...."

"'Convinced them'?" Delia echoed.

"That's all he would say, but he didn't sound like he approved of whatever their tactics were. The Yankees sold the property back to the bank and left."

Delia stared at the unfinished house, which was big enough to hold four or even more buildings the size of the parsonage, then back at Jude. "So you're saying that I—"

"Might be able to buy this place for a very fair price. It's not completed, obviously, so it would be a while until you could move in, but that's also its great advantage, Delia. You could have it finished to your own specifications."

Delia felt a rising sense of excitement. "So I could…" she murmured, continuing to gaze at the building. "Oh, Jude, could I see the inside?"

Jude grinned. "I rather thought you'd want to." Setting the brake, he stepped down from the wagon and held out his hand to assist her. She took it, feeling the calluses of hard manual work.

Too exhilarated to be ladylike, Delia ran the few yards into the house. Inside, there were no room divisions, only a rock chimney on one side and a plank stairway in the middle that led to the second story.

"This could be the drawing room," she said, pointing to the chimney side of the first floor. "And the kitchen, back there, and perhaps a parlor, over there," she added, gesturing in each direction in turn. "Can we go upstairs?" she asked.

Jude, clearly pleased at her enthusiasm, offered his hand again. "Allow me to assist you, ma'am. In place of this," he said, indicating the rough-hewn railing, "you could have a polished pecanwood banister and stairs."

"Oh, Jude," she said, as they reached the top. "This is so wonderful. Why, there's room for at least *six* bedrooms up here, even if I make mine large." She gazed out one of the framed openings for a window and gave a laugh of pure joy as she took in the view of the Llano River flowing close by, the rolling, tree-dotted countryside beyond it and the blue hills in the distance.

"You want it, don't you?" he said, as they descended the stairs once more. It was more a statement than a question.

Delia paused. "Can I...can I afford it?" she wondered aloud. Jude knew the amount of her inheritance.

Jude said, "I believe so, but of course you should think about it carefully."

"And pray about it, my grandpa would say," she mused.

Jude nodded.

Delia closed her eyes. She could imagine living here—no more leaky roof and drafts and the parties she could hold here, with guests spending the night upstairs if they chose. And someday, maybe some of the bedrooms would hold her children... *But who would be her husband—and their father?*

What would Charles say about this place? She imagined showing it to him. When she had spoken about wanting to buy a house, he had suggested she wait and let a husband provide it for her. Would he change his stance on the subject when he saw this place?

She felt a blush creeping up her neck and looked away from Jude. She felt so confused. She had been attracted to Jude on the day they met, but he had actively discouraged her on that score. Yet he had found this place for her. Charles, meanwhile, had made it clear that he was quite interested in her. If only she knew what Jude had been thinking about her kiss and what would have happened next.

"I'll have to meet with Mr. Dawson," she thought aloud, gazing at the unfinished house. "If after meeting with him, he confirms I can afford it—considering the cost of finishing it, too, of course—I'll take it."

"Very businesslike, Delia," Jude said.

"My grandfather had always taught me to count the cost of a project before beginning it," she replied modestly, but then had a sudden thought. "Speaking of which, where on earth will I find someone to finish this place for me?"

Jude grinned innocently. "Well...I *am* a carpenter. And the work I'm doing for the Hestons won't take much longer—"

"You could do this all by yourself?"

"There's some parts I might have to find a couple of fellows to help me with," he agreed. "But that shouldn't be hard."

"So finding this place for me was a scheme to get work?" Delia asked. She was unable to subdue a pang of disappointment that this might have been his sole motive.

His eyes under his broad-brimmed hat were hooded, unreadable in the bright sunlight. "Seemed to me I could kill two birds with one stone," he said. "I found a source of employment—a reason to stay for a spell, rather than riding on—and something you were wanting, Delia."

Delia resolved to go to the bank this very day and speak to Amos Dawson and get the paperwork started if he thought it was feasible for her. And she would speak to God about it, too, when she said her bedtime prayers.

"How soon could you finish it?" she asked as they got back into the wagon and headed back toward her house. "The only difficulty would be if the deacons find a new pastor before you do—but I suppose if that happened I could take a room in the hotel for a time."

"It's September now. With good weather, I reckon you could be in there by Thanksgiving, maybe sooner," Jude said.

Another thought came to her as they rolled along.

"I think with some of my money I'll pay for some improvements to the old place, and you could do those, too. A new preacher and his family deserve a new roof and new paint throughout, at the very least."

Jude looked at her with approval. "You are quite a generous lady, Delia Keller. Quite a lady indeed."

After checking on Miss Susan, whose spirits seemed a bit brighter than they had been earlier, Delia decided to go straight to the bank. No one else had any interest in the half-finished house, as far as she knew, but she didn't want to take any chance of losing it to another buyer. That house was meant to be hers.

Amos Dawson was pleased to see her, judging by the promptness with which she was ushered into his private office by the same wispy young teller who, before the news of her fortune, had acted as if her entering the bank was an imposition. Now, before leaving Delia with Dawson, he offered Delia a glass of lemonade and freshly baked cookies. Delia accepted both with a gracious smile.

"Miss Keller, how might the Llano Crossing Bank serve your needs today?" Dawson said, beaming after the teller had left them alone.

Delia told him of her interest in the Delacey place, without mentioning how she had learned of it.

"Ah, splendid!" the banker cried, clapping his hands together. "The property would be eminently suitable for you, Miss Keller."

"It would be if the price is right," Delia responded, injecting briskness into her voice. It wouldn't be wise to show just how much she wanted the place. "I've no intention of being foolish with my money."

"Of course not," Dawson responded, his face bland as buttermilk. He took up a sheet of paper and, dipping a pen into the inkwell above his blotter, scratched something on it and handed the sheet across the desk to Delia. "This is what the bank is owed for the property and the house."

Delia, studying the amount he had written, was careful to keep her features as blank as the paper had been moments before. Sure the cost had been inflated at least a little, she named a sum several hundred dollars less.

Mr. Dawson hesitated. "You drive a hard bargain, Miss Keller, but it's been on the bank's books for a long time. Very well, the bank accepts your offer."

Delia just smiled. "Excellent."

"We'll begin drawing up the papers immediately," Dawson went on. "I'm delighted you are planning on remaining in Llano Crossing. Oh, and may I suggest a group of fine German craftsmen from Gillespie Springs to finish your house?"

"Thank you," Delia said, "but I have someone in mind already for that." She saw a curious gleam in the banker's eyes and decided not to satisfy it. "He thought I would be able to move in by Thanksgiving, if all goes well."

"Of course, you may not have acquired all your furnishings by then," the banker pointed out. "It'll take time to select quality pieces and have them shipped to Llano Crossing."

"I had thought of seeing what Mr. Dean had at the mercantile," she said aloud, while wondering if Jude's talents included furniture-making.

Dawson sniffed his disdain. "As a stopgap measure, perhaps. But I am in touch with craftsmen who know how to make furniture fit for a lady in your position. Why, I've even assisted Mrs. Ladley in such purchases."

"I'll keep that in mind," Delia murmured noncommittally. She would have to be careful not to place herself too thoroughly in Dawson's hands or she would drain her legacy in a matter of months.

She rose. "Thank you, Mr. Dawson. When will the papers be ready for my signature?"

"Tomorrow, Miss Keller. Shall we say nine?"

Delia nodded, already thinking ahead. After she signed, she might do some of that shopping she had been contemplating.

"Oh, and there's another matter you might give some consideration," he added before she could reach the door.

Delia turned back reluctantly. Property, workmen, lodging, furnishings—didn't she have enough to ponder already?

"Investments," he said, scuttling toward her as if he feared she might take wing before he could utter the word. "You must consider putting the balance of your money to work for you, so it can grow. There are a myriad of ways—stocks, real estate, and the Committee for Civic Improvement has been investigating some ways of improving the town as a whole."

"Of course," she said, feeling her head beginning to ache. Her life had been so uncomplicated before this.

He must have seen that she was growing weary. "But I have taken enough of your time, Miss Keller. There is no need to discuss such a detailed subject today. Once construction of your house is under way, and you can spare me an hour or so, perhaps then…"

"Certainly, Mr. Dawson," she said, and made her escape before he could bring up anything else.

Outside, she was surprised to find Charles Ladley sitting in his landau, as if he were waiting for her.

"I saw you go in," he said, taking off his hat to mop his brow. "I must say, I didn't think you'd be in there as long as that. Conducting weighty business, Miss Keller?"

"You might say so," she said with a wink. "Charles, if you have time, I want to show you something."

He looked intrigued. "My carriage is at your disposal, milady," he said, reaching down a hand to assist her to get in.

Minutes later, they reached the site. "I'm buying this place," she told him. "That's why I was at the bank. Would you like to see the inside?"

"Of course." He followed her into the building, listening impassively as she described what she planned to do with it. Leaning heavily on his cane, he followed her up the crude stairway to see the upper floor, gazing in all directions, admiring the view as she had.

"It's perfect for me, don't you think?"

"It could be pleasant, once a lot of work is done," he said. "How did you find it?"

Delia had known the question would come. She knew she could just say she'd been out exploring and come across it, but it wasn't in her to lie. "Jude Tucker thought I might like it," she said, watching him carefully to see how he would react.

His jaw hardened and his expressive eyes went flat. "Oh? So you've been confiding your dreams to Tucker, have you?"

He was hurt, she thought with a guilty pang. "I

wouldn't say that," she said carefully. "He's looking for work, and he knew I was in the market for a house, that's all." She wouldn't blush if she didn't think about how she had told Jude of her need on her shadowy porch at midnight.

"I see."

"It could be done by Thanksgiving, he thinks. But I'll need your advice in choosing furniture and drapery and such things," she added, hoping that would appeal to him, "since most of the furniture in the parsonage is pretty old and worn. The only difficulty will be if the church board finds a new pastor before the house is finished, but I could take a room at the hotel." She became aware she was chattering to fill the heavy silence.

"You know you can count on my assistance," he said. "And you must do as you please, of course. But it all seems so unnecessary."

She blinked, uncertain of his meaning.

"My parents wouldn't hear of your staying alone at a hotel when we have several guest rooms at Ladley House," he explained impatiently. "You could move in tomorrow, if you wanted. And you should. It's hardly fitting that you stay in that tumbledown old shack in the current circumstances."

Delia opened her mouth to defend the old parsonage. She knew every nook and cranny of it. It had known all her grandpa's and her joys and sorrows and had been home to them for many years. It wasn't such an awful place. But soon it wouldn't be hers anymore.

Charles raised a hand and went on. "Don't you see, if you moved into Ladley House, we could spend more time together—all under strictly proper circumstances. I—I hadn't meant to speak about it so soon, with you in mourning, but I have great hopes for a future with you. And I had thought that finding a house would be something we did *together*."

Chapter Eleven

She couldn't stifle her gasp. "I—I didn't realize you were thinking of such things.…" She felt as if she were being swept along in the middle of the Llano River at floodstage.

Charles looked crestfallen. "I think I've tried to move things along too fast, Delia. It's a failing I have. I'm sorry."

The sight of his downcast face distracted Delia from her doubts. "Oh, Charles, I'm not saying no. It's just… just too soon for me to make such a big decision."

Charles smiled unexpectedly. "Delia, you are as wise as you are beautiful. And brave and hospitable, too. It's kind of you to offer shelter to Miss Susan."

Shelter? He seemed to know more than what she had told him and his parents on Sunday.

"I saw Dixon Miller earlier today, and he mentioned the sheriff had spoken to him about his cowhand Donley Morrison," Charles explained. "Does she plan to stay with you long? Mightn't they reconcile sooner if… if she wasn't avoiding him?"

He couldn't know the whole story if he was asking

that, she reasoned. "What she's avoiding are his fists, Charles—and his demands for her money so he can buy whiskey."

He looked shocked. "I see. Very well, but be careful, won't you? Men who would abuse their wives are dangerous, and they wouldn't scruple at harming those who try to stop them, either."

Delia and Miss Susan were just doing their dinner dishes the next night when Jude showed up at her door.

"Evening, Delia. Miss Susan, how're you feeling, ma'am?"

Delia saw the older woman's face turn pink with appreciation that he'd asked.

"Better, on the whole. It's fascinating watching this—" she indicated her bruised eye, which she could now open "—turning from black to purple to green," she said with a wry twist to her lips. "I think I'll go back to work tomorrow, just for the pleasure of watching folks goggle at it."

"That's the spirit." Jude smiled. "Delia, I brought these drawings over for you to see." He handed her several sheets of paper with detailed drawings of how he planned to finish her house and a sketch of the house as he imagined it would look from the outside when completed. It was obvious he'd put considerable thought into it, and she said so.

"Make any changes you'd like," Jude said, gesturing toward the drawing. "It's going to be *your* house, after all."

"Well, how about a larger window, here," she said, pointing to the parlor area. "And could there be a veranda?"

"You're the boss, ma'am," he said agreeably. "I'll be finished with what I'm doing for the Hestons by the end of the week, so I can start immediately after that. I'm going to be staying with them, at least till Mr. Heston's arm is fully mended, so you can let me know if you think of anything else."

After Miss Susan had admired his work also, she excused herself, saying she had some mending to do, leaving Jude and Delia together on the porch.

There was a pleasant breeze, with a hint of coolness to the air, now that the heat of the day was over. Fall was indeed imminent.

Jude felt in no hurry to leave, and Delia seemed pleased at that. The silence between them was companionable.

"Jude, what was your occupation?" Delia asked, after a while. "Before the war, I mean. Did you work as a carpenter then?"

Jude sighed, his eyes on the rolling blue hills just visible over the tops of the mesquite trees. He'd figured Delia would get around to this question eventually, and he cared too much about her to try to fob her off with some vague answer.

"You don't have to tell me," Delia said, before Jude could speak. "If you'd rather not. It's not polite to pry. You just didn't seem like you're running from the law or anything."

"No, I'm no desperado on the loose," Jude said, smiling to show her he didn't mind her asking. *I'm just running from myself.*

"Nor like some man who left a wife and seven children back East," Delia added.

Jude's smile broadened. "No, I didn't do that, either. I've never been married—nor a father." He sighed again, shifting his gaze to the drawings she still held. "All right, but I have to say before I tell you anything more—that part of my life is over now."

Delia lifted her hands in a gesture to indicate Jude's terms were understood.

"I learned carpentry at my father's knee, but then I became a preacher," Jude said. "I had a church in the little town of Mount Mulberry, Tennessee."

Delia's eyes flew open in astonishment. She seemed to be waiting for him to say something else, but when he didn't, she finally asked, "So why aren't you one now?"

Jude thought about the blood and noise and the senseless losses of a battle. And he thought of Nora and the way she'd scarred his soul. He wanted to be honest with Delia, but she'd never look at him the same if she knew. And some pains were just too private to expose.

"War changes a man," he said at last, hoping Delia would leave it at that. "I've done things that make going back to preaching impossible."

He saw puzzlement cloud her green eyes. "But, Jude, the Lord will forgive anything. The Bible says so. You just have to ask Him."

"I have. And I believe He's forgiven me. But…" *But I can't forgive myself.*

Delia gave him an exasperated look. "Jude, the pulpit's standing empty right here in Llano Crossing."

"I told you, that part of my life is over."

"I don't mean being a carpenter can't be serving the Lord, too," she said, her tone conciliatory. "Jesus was a carpenter, after all."

"Besides," Jude argued, "I thought you said the

mayor was taking over the preaching until a preacher could be found."

Delia looked down at her hands for a moment. "Mr. Ladley tries, but he's no pastor—which you would know if you came to church," she finished tartly, her eyes returning to his. "Why weren't you there Sunday? Maybe if you came it would give you a calling for it again."

Now it was Jude's turn to look away. Mr. Heston had asked Jude to attend with them yesterday, but he'd declined with some vague excuse. But there was some truth in Delia's last words, too—Jude was afraid that, inside the sanctuary in the midst of a church service, he'd feel that desire to preach the Word again, only to know he was no longer worthy.

And he hadn't liked the possibility that he'd see Delia Keller sitting with the mayor's son.

"Okay," said Delia, when he said nothing more, "but please consider coming next Sunday."

Her appeal made him suddenly irresolute. He wanted to please her, but what would be the outcome?

"Maybe I will," he said.

"Knowing you were a preacher explains a lot," Delia said, surprising him. "Your compassion with Miss Susan, for example. I imagine you were very good at it—at pastoring, I mean."

He had been, until war had challenged his basic assumptions about the goodness of men—and his own ability to withstand temptation.

"Please...you won't tell anyone what I told you, will you?" he said.

She sighed. "All right, but I warn you, I'm going to be praying that you feel the calling again," Delia informed him. "After you finish my house, of course," she added with a smile.

She was going to pray about him. The idea mattered to him more than he wanted it to.

"I hope you're praying for rain, while you're at it. We could use some," he said lightly, to defuse her seriousness. He nodded toward the dried grass in her yard.

"That's a good man," Miss Susan murmured, coming back onto the porch after Jude had ridden off in direction of town. "He's worth ten of Charles Ladley."

Delia wondered if she'd overheard what he'd told her, but Miss Susan didn't seem the type to eavesdrop.

"You've met Jude...what, three times now? What makes you say that?" Delia asked, not in an argumentative way, but in a tone that showed she really wanted to know.

"It's something a body can just *tell,* that's all. Especially when you get to be my age."

"I think Charles is a good man, too," Delia put in mildly. "He's been very kind to me—not only him but all his family. I've liked him all my life—and at last he seems to like me, too." She wondered what Miss Susan would say if she knew Charles had asked her to stay with his family so they could get to know each other better, all but saying it was a prelude to marriage—and that he said he preferred that they buy a house together someday soon.

"Humph!" Miss Susan snorted. "There's kind and there's kind that expects to *get.* I don't like to tell you your business, Delia. Just look deep, before you make up your mind."

"Make up my mind?" Delia repeated. "Jude's made

it perfectly clear that he's not interested in me that way or in settling here. I need a house, and he wants work. It's as simple as that. And Charles and I have more in common now..."

Miss Susan put her hands on her hips. "Jude Tucker's not *interested*? Delia Keller, open your eyes! He may say he's not, but look at what he *does*."

Delia could only stare at her while Miss Susan's words echoed in her soul. "I'll think about it," she promised.

"I wish Reverend McKinney were still here. He'd tell you the same thing I am. And you know he'd tell you to pray about it."

"I wish he were here, too," Delia said bleakly and not only because of those two men.

"How's your courtship of the lovely young Delia going?" Charles Ladley, senior, asked his son over port and cigars in a private room off the hotel's dining room. "Things moving right along?"

Soon the other members of the Committee for Civic Improvement would be walking in, but for now it was pleasant to lean back and chat with his father after a sumptuous meal.

The younger Charles grinned at his father through a haze of aromatic blue smoke. "It's going well, I'd say. Of course, I'm having to proceed slowly," he admitted, thinking of their conversation after he'd seen the house she was buying, "her bein' a preacher's granddaughter and all. Don't want to spook the filly before she's saddled—with matrimony—do I?" He didn't want his father to know how he'd nearly scared Delia away by pressuring her too soon.

The elder Ladley chuckled at the image. "Boy, you're a chip off the old block, indeed you are! But don't go *too* slow and let some other man catch her eye. Be a little bold. The ladies like that, now and again."

His son quirked a brow. "What do you suggest, Father?"

The mayor blew a smoke ring and thought about it for a long moment.

"An expensive gift might be just the thing. Something so valuable she knows she really shouldn't accept it since you're not betrothed but something so delightful that she really can't bear to let it go."

Charles was hesitant. "But don't we need to save money for...our project? It doesn't seem the time to be spending—"

"Boy, sometimes you have to spend money to make money, haven't I taught you that? If you can gull that girl into marrying you—the sooner the better—we'll have even more money to achieve our goal than if we only fleece the town, you see?"

Father and son smiled together in perfect accord.

"Hmm...I think I've thought of the perfect thing," Charles murmured.

Chapter Twelve

"That was such fun, Charles!" Delia said a few days later, as they walked their mounts back to town to cool them down after an exhilarating gallop on the road south of town. "I'd forgotten how wonderful it felt to go so fast and feel the wind in my hair! I felt like I was flying!" She reached down and patted the glossy neck of the gelding she'd borrowed from the Ladley stables.

"You're a natural horsewoman," Charles praised. "Even though you weren't used to a sidesaddle."

"You're very tactful—and Midnight's very forgiving of my rustiness," she said, patting the horse again. "Papa used to take me up on his horse, and we never told Mama how fast we'd go, but after he left all I had to ride was Grandpa's mule that passed on long ago."

"Mother told me to tell you to keep her riding habit and the hat, since she doesn't ride much anymore. The habit fits as if it were made for you," he added, his gaze frankly admiring.

"How kind of her!" Delia said, flushing with his praise. She was aware that the habit emphasized her trim waist and that the deep green hue flattered her coloring.

"Sure you won't change your mind and come back to the house for a cold drink?" Charles coaxed, as they drew up in front of the mercantile. "Cook makes the best iced tea in Texas, and Manuel got fresh ice from the ice house this morning."

"I'd like to, but now that I've played this morning when I should be planning for the new house, I'd better stop in here as I'd planned," she told him, handing him the reins and dismounting. "Oh! I'd forgotten how stiff one gets when one doesn't ride often!" she said, self-conscious about the awkward way she was walking.

"We can soon remedy that," he told her. "You have to remember, you're a lady of leisure now."

"Wonder if you'd mind goin' with Lucy on some errands?" Heston said that morning. "She had her heart set on gettin' supplies at the general store today—says she's out a' flour an' cornmeal an' everything, but Doc Jones says my arm won't be ready t' carry loads for a spell."

Jude had pronounced the room addition finished just an hour ago, and he'd actually planned to visit the mill and check out their lumber supply that morning, but it could wait till later. "Just let me stick my head under the pump handle." He was hot from his exertions, and he hadn't shaved, but he supposed he looked respectable enough to be seen with Mrs. Heston.

Once they'd picked up supplies at the general store, though, Mrs. Heston confessed that she also had a hankering to visit the mercantile and perhaps then the seamstress's shop. She hadn't had a new Sunday go-to-meetin' dress in five years, and her eyes were getting too bad to sew her own.

Jude groaned inwardly as he lifted the brown-wrapped packages and prepared to follow Mrs. Heston to the mercantile, realizing that by the time they'd visited two more places, the mill might be closed. He'd learned it closed at noon on Friday. He'd hoped to have the wood and other supplies delivered Saturday morning, but he reminded himself how good the Hestons had been to him, providing him with a roof over his head and three square meals a day. He could go to the mill on Saturday morning and maybe even talk Barton Jeffers into delivering the same day.

Jude climbed up the three stone stairs to the boardwalk, following Mrs. Heston, and stepped into the mercantile.

"Why, look who's here, Jude!" Mrs. Heston's voice rang out before his eyes had even adjusted from the bright sunlight to the pleasant dimness inside the store. "Just look who I've found in here!"

Delia shifted her gaze from the shorter Mrs. Heston to the lean figure backlit by the doorway. He strode toward them, his boot heels thudding on the flooring.

She was surprised to feel her pulse accelerate. Goodness, she had forgotten Jude Tucker was so tall—he had to be at least a head taller than Charles. She felt almost tiny as he stopped in front of her, those pale wolf eyes studying her as his mouth relaxed into a smile.

"Looks like you're too late, Mrs. Heston," he said in that gravelly voice of his. "Miss Keller's already bought out the store." He gestured toward the mound of parcels of various sizes and shapes, to which Mr. Dean, the proprietor, was still adding. There was also a carved wooden vanity table and matching stool that stood next to Delia, which she had apparently purchased as well.

Mrs. Heston chuckled.

Delia smiled back at Jude. "Oh, no, I've only bought a few things I've been needing," she said, trying to keep her voice light and carefree. She couldn't imagine why this man affected her the way he did—his appearance was so rough and uncouth next to Charles's polished gentility. From what she had seen, Charles never had left his house unless he was immaculately groomed.

Today, unshaven and dressed in a worn shirt and trousers, Jude Tucker looked almost dangerous—like an outlaw on the run.

"I see you've been riding, dear," Mrs. Heston was saying, gesturing toward the riding habit Delia was wearing.

Jude peered over his shoulders to the empty hitching rail outside. "Where's your horse? I didn't know you had one—did you just buy it?"

"No, Charles loaned me one of their geldings, and he took him back to their stable," Delia explained, not missing the way Jude's smile faded, his eyes becoming remote, wintry.

She turned back to Mrs. Heston. "I'd forgotten how enjoyable it was!" she went on. "I think I'll have to make a good saddle horse one of my next purchases."

"I'm sure Jude could help you with that," Mrs. Heston told her, beaming at Jude. "That Shiloh of his is so gentle for a stallion. Why, he eats sugar lumps right from my hand."

"She's spoiled him for good—me, too, for that matter," Jude said, though his smile somehow didn't reach his eyes as he looked at Delia. "They've made me so welcome, it'll be hard to leave when it's time to go back West."

"Well, *we* hope he'll never leave," Mrs. Heston put in. "He's become indispensable to Jim and me—like the son we never had."

Jude was clearly touched by the old woman's praise, Delia noted, but then Mrs. Heston was speaking again and Delia was forced to wrest her gaze from Jude.

"I hear you bought the old Delacey place, Delia, and Jude's going to finish it for you."

"Yes, it's going to be wonderful. A palace, compared to the parsonage. I still have to pinch myself to make sure I'm not dreaming!"

"How exciting, Delia! I'm sure your grandpa would be so pleased for you," Mrs. Heston gushed. "Or I should say, I *know* he's lookin' down from Heaven, and he's tickled p—"

Delia wanted to beat a hasty retreat from the now grim-faced man in front of her. Seeing that Mr. Dean had finished wrapping her purchases, she interrupted the older lady's flow. "Yes, I'm sure you're right. But I mustn't hold you up, Mrs. Heston," Delia said. "Give your husband my best."

"And how are you planning on getting all those things home, Delia?" Mrs. Heston asked. "You can't possibly carry all that."

"I'm not. Mr. Dean is going to deliver it. Of course, he can't do that until he closes at the end of the day—"

"Nonsense," Lucy Heston cut in. "Jude could borrow the wagon to take those things now, couldn't he, Mr. Dean?"

The mercantile owner agreed.

"You go on with Jude, Delia. I know Jude's bored to death, keeping an old woman company."

"But what about your purchases, Mrs. Heston?" Delia asked, not at all certain she wanted to be alone with Jude after his disapproving looks.

"I still need to visit Miss Susan's, and Mr. Dean will hold those things till you come back. Take your time, mind," she added, when Jude looked as if he was going to protest.

"But, Mrs. Heston, it's not necessary, really," Delia said. If Jude didn't want to help her, she certainly didn't want his assistance—Lucy Heston didn't know what she was getting Delia into.

"It's no problem, dear," Mrs. Heston insisted, and Delia was sure she saw a twinkle of mischief in the old woman's eyes.

Jude said nothing throughout the process of loading the buckboard and wordlessly assisted Delia to climb aboard. Nor did it seem like he planned to speak on the short drive back to the parsonage.

"Nice weather we're having," she said at last, desperate to break the silence. "Mild for September…"

"I reckon."

She was going to have to be more direct. "I—I'm sorry Mrs. Heston got you into this," Delia said, "even though it'll be nice not having to wait on the things to be delivered."

"It's nothing." He unloaded her purchases and brought them into the house with the same silent efficiency as when he had loaded them onto the wagon. Finally he wiped his brow with his handkerchief.

"That's it, then." He took a step toward the door.

"Would you like some cold lemonade from the

springhouse?" Delia offered, then wondered why she was trying to delay his leaving. He'd done her the favor he had come to do.

"There's no need to trouble yourself, Delia." His gaze was fixed at some point slightly above her head.

"It's the least I can do to thank you for helping me get these things home," she said.

He shrugged. "All right, if you're sure it's no trouble. And if you're sure Charles Ladley won't mind," he added, those pale eyes on hers.

At first she couldn't believe he had said it.

She felt a spark of anger. "Why would Charles mind me offering a glass of cold lemonade to a friend who did me a favor?"

He shrugged, avoiding Delia's gaze.

"Charles doesn't own me. He's a *friend,* too."

His head snapped up at that. "Oh, he wants to be much more than your friend."

"What's that supposed to mean?"

"Has he asked you to marry him, Delia?"

Delia felt herself blushing, furious with Jude for asking because she couldn't exactly say no—Charles *had* admitted he was looking forward to a future with her. "It's much too soon for me to be thinking of such a thing—even if I weren't in mourning," she reminded him, with a pointed glance at her black dress. She was angry at herself, too, for blushing, knowing that Jude would take that for an admission, no matter what she said.

"Taking refuge in vagueness, Delia?" His words were like a slap.

She gave him a bitter laugh. "I guess you won't care if he courts me since you *won't!*"

The gleam in his eyes went dangerous. "I'll show you how much I 'don't care,' Delia," he said, then crossed the room in two quick strides, catching her face between his two hands and kissing her until neither of them could breathe. Delia was too shocked to struggle.

Then he let her go just as quickly, and all they could do was stare at one another while they tried in vain to catch their breath.

Jude looked just as angry as he had looked before.

Finally, Delia drew herself up in icy dignity. "Perhaps that lemonade wouldn't be a good idea after all."

Jude had gone very still. "I reckon not, Miss Keller. Please excuse me." He stalked toward the door, grabbing his hat up off the table where he'd left it.

She whirled away from him, praying she wouldn't start crying before he was gone.

Chapter Thirteen

"Well, ain't that a nice sight," commented James Heston, coming into the tackroom that Jude used as his room in the barn. Jude looked up from the Bible that lay open on his knees.

In the week since his confrontation with Delia, he'd kept busy with odd jobs for the Hestons and their friends around town. But he hadn't done anything further about buying the lumber for Delia's house, nor had she sent word that she'd found someone else for the job. Pretty soon he would be out of excuses for remaining in Llano Crossing.

Every time he dreamed, it was of Delia Keller, her green eyes hot with anger at him. Charles Ladley was always present, sometimes smirking in the background, sometimes with his arm around Delia. In the illogical way of dreams, all three of them stood at the pulpit of the Llano Crossing Church. On the pulpit, where the open Bible usually lay, was a coiled rattlesnake. Seemingly Delia couldn't see her danger because she leaned trustingly into Ladley, just inches from the snake, and told Jude to go away.

At this point Jude would wake up, drenched in a cold sweat, and sleep was over for the night.

It had been during these predawn morning hours that he'd dug out the worn leather-covered Bible that had lain forgotten in the bottom of his saddlebag for so long. He'd begun to read it again and had been doing so when his boss entered.

"Yessir, that purely is a beautiful sight, you readin' the Good Book," Heston said again, nodding at the Bible in Jude's lap. "Maybe this is a good time t' ask you the same thing I ask you at the end of every week."

Jude feigned confusion, though he knew what was coming.

"Are you goin' to go to church with the missus an' me on Sunday mornin', or are you gonna stay here like a heathen? An' don't be tellin' me you've got jobs t' make up because of the rain, neither."

Jude took a deep breath. Maybe it was time.

"All right, you win," he said and a sudden lightness within him told him he'd made the right decision.

"Well, hallelujah!" Heston cried. "Wait'll I tell Lucy!"

Then both men became aware of a sound, or rather the absence of a sound. It had stopped raining, and now a beam of sunlight came lancing through the window next to Jude's bunk.

Jude studied it. Well, if he was going to go to Sunday worship in the morning, there was something he had to do now. He'd just been reading the part of the Gospels where it said something about mending one's fences before taking one's gift to the altar.

"Think I'll take a walk," he said.

* * *

Delia, her brown curls pinned up under by a scrap of calico folded triangularly into a kerchief, hummed as she dived into the deep cleaning that had never gotten done this spring because of her grandfather's illness. She hadn't wanted Miss Susan to feel like she had to offer to help, but once she had walked Miss Susan to the shop, it had seemed like a good day to tackle the job at last. There hadn't been any news of a new preacher coming, but if she suddenly had to move into a hotel, having this chore done would make the move that much easier.

And it would keep her—at least for a few hours—from wondering what she ought to do about her new house. She had received no word from Jude after their angry parting last week. She had no idea whether he still planned to finish it for her or not. She'd thought, perhaps, he had even left town, until Miss Susan had mentioned seeing him enlarging the corral at Mr. Pierce's livery.

Delia knew she ought to walk down to the Hestons' and ask him point-blank whether he was going to complete the house or not, so if he wasn't, she could go ahead and hire the German workers from Gillespie Springs Mr. Dawson had suggested. Was she being a coward? All she knew right now was that her dusty closets were a lot more appealing than braving those cold gray-blue eyes of Jude's. Maybe tomorrow she'd be up to the task. She had to know sooner or later, after all.

"Anyone home?" called a deep male voice from the front door, just as she started back to work.

Charles had mentioned something about a ride, but he hadn't said when, exactly, and she didn't think it was him. The voice was too deep, too gravelly... *Too like Jude Tucker's.* But Jude wouldn't come here, after the way they had left matters between them.

"I'm coming—"

It *was* Jude Tucker standing there, looking completely different from the unshaven cowhand who had left her home so precipitately after their harsh words. He wore a fresh shirt and clean denim trousers, and he appeared to have stopped at the Barber and Bath shop in town, for he smelled faintly of soap. Even his boots looked freshly brushed, she noted absently. In one hand he held his broad-brimmed hat; in the other, he held a small bouquet of wildflowers, though where he'd found them in the early September heat she had no idea.

"Hello," he said, and held out the bouquet. "Did I catch you at a bad time?"

Those light gray-blue eyes roamed over her kerchief and old dress, and she felt sure there must be as many smudges of dust on her cheeks as there were on her dress.

"N-no, it's...it's all right," she stammered and took the bouquet with hands that were visibly shaking.

"It's a peace offering."

She looked from him to the flowers and back again. "Uh...th-thank you. Come in. But that wasn't...n-necessary," she said.

"I thought it was. You might want to put those in water," he suggested, crossing her threshold.

"I will...."

"You're in the middle of cleaning," he said. "You're busy. I won't stay."

He looked as though he was going to turn around and leave. "No, come in and have that lemonade I owe you," she said quickly, gesturing for him to enter and smiling to show that she had forgiven him. "Cleaning is thirsty work, and I was just getting ready to take a break." She reached for a pair of glasses in her cupboard. "Sit down, please," she said, indicating the kitchen table. "I just have to go out to the springhouse and get the pitcher."

When she returned, she poured them each a glass of the cold liquid and then watched as he took a sip.

"I've been trying to decide what to keep and what to leave for a new preacher," she said, pointing at the furniture, once again feeling she had to fill the silence. "Most of these things are still good, and preachers never seem to have much. I'm buying mostly new things, just taking the things that had been my mother's. Of course, if he came soon, I'd have to put some of these things in storage at Mr. Pierce's livery. Mrs. Purvis next door would take the chickens. It'd be so odd not to wake up to the rooster crowing...."

He let her talk, saying nothing, just watching her.

She had a sudden pang of fear at his silence. "Are you—that is, did you come to tell me you were leaving? That you aren't going to finish my house?"

Jude looked down at his hands. "I wasn't sure if you still wanted me to," he admitted.

"Of course I do."

He seemed to take encouragement to speak from that. "I...I wanted to apologize," he said. "I was out of line when I was here last week."

Delia gathered her courage. "Are you apologizing for kissing me, Jude? Because I don't want you to— apologize, that is. I think I'd like to try it again—kissing—only not with you angry at me." Then she held her breath to see what he would do.

She only had to wonder for the space of a few heart-beats. Then he was out of his chair and kneeling in front of hers, then he kissed her again, and this time he was definitely *not* angry. While he kissed her, he pulled off her kerchief and somehow the pins got loose and her curls were cascading around her neck.

"I've wanted to touch your hair for so long," he murmured, raising his head just long enough to say the words before his lips touched hers again.

Then a knock sounded at the front door, and they sprang apart.

Jude's eyes bored into Delia's. "You expecting someone?"

"No. Yes. I—I don't know," she said, suddenly flustered. Charles would have questions about Jude Tucker's presence there—especially if he saw the flowers. She was not about to try to hide them, though, not with Jude watching. They lay where she had left them on the kitchen table, near where she had been sitting.

"I'll just go see who…" Her voice trailed off as she walked quickly down the hall away from the kitchen.

As she'd feared, it was Charles.

"Why, hello, Delia, whatever have you been doing?" He studied her messy hair and her rumpled appearance with amusement, but his eyes slitted when he spotted Jude coming down the hall from the kitchen.

"I've been cleaning," she explained again. "Charles, you remember Jude Tucker…"

"Tucker," Charles said tightly, nodding. His knuckles had tightened around his cane.

Jude nodded back. "Ladley."

Delia sensed that Charles was waiting to be informed about what Tucker was doing here, but she felt she had told him enough already. Oh, glory, she could smell the flowers clear out here in the parlor.

"I was just leaving," Jude said at last. "As I said, Miss Delia, I'll be buying the lumber tomorrow and starting to work on the house bright and early Monday."

"That will be fine. Goodbye, Jude."

Delia watched Charles watch through the window as Jude strode down the steps. He smiled with a certain grim satisfaction at one point, and after the sound of retreating hoofbeats he turned back to Delia.

"I have a surprise for you, Delia. Too bad Tucker saw it before you did, but come look."

Puzzled, and still shaking a little from the feeling of an averted confrontation, Delia came to the window and looked where Ladley was pointing.

Next to where Charles's bay saddle horse was tied to the back of the Ladley carriage stood a tall coal-black horse. It pawed the ground restively. On its back sat a lady's sidesaddle.

"She's a thoroughbred, Delia," Charles told her. "She's yours. Go put on your riding habit, and you can try out her paces."

Delia felt her jaw drop in astonishment. "Mine? But, Charles, I couldn't possibly accept such a gift.…" But she was already flying out the doorway, and a moment later she was stroking the mare's inky, velvety muzzle. "Oh, you're *beautiful,*" she breathed, inhaling the mare's scent.

"Her name is Zephyr, though you can rename her anything you want, naturally," Charles said. "And of course you can accept her. In your position, you'll need a mount worthy of you."

Could she find the words to refuse this wonderful

creature? The mare seemed to be trying to persuade her by butting her shoulder.

"Charles, I have nowhere to keep a horse."

"You'll keep her in our stable, of course, until you move to your new house."

"How do you know I'm a good enough rider for a horse like this?" she asked him. There was a hint of fire and mischief in the mare's eyes, a promise of speed in the supple muscles that rippled under Delia's hand as she stroked the mare's high shoulder.

"You've seemed a competent enough horsewoman when we've gone riding," Charles told her. "And having a horse like this will make you even more so in a short time."

Delia studied the mare as she considered his words. She and Charles had gone riding several times, early in the morning when it was still cool, and she'd loved flying over the roads on the borrowed gelding. But he was docile and perfectly trained. She knew she had a lot to learn about riding a horse like this spirited creature.

"Darling Delia, please say you'll accept her," Charles pleaded, the entreaty in his dark eyes weakening her rapidly melting resolve. "You know you want to."

She took a step back from the mare and from Charles. "But what would it signify to you?" she asked, amazed at her own temerity.

Ladley seemed to struggle to formulate an answer. At last he said, "As much or as little as you want it to, Delia."

"That's clear as mud."

He smiled down at her. "At the very least, a demonstration of my regard for you."

"And at most?"

"A betrothal present. But only if you want it to be," he added quickly, as she opened her mouth to protest.

"I...I couldn't," she said. "I'm sorry. I'm not ready for that, not yet. I'll enjoy riding her, but I think she should remain yours unless—"

"Say 'until,'" he interrupted, but his face remained bland and unconcerned. "All right, Delia. You're a prudent lady. I saw her, and I just wanted you to have her, regardless of whether *I'm* part of the gift or not. I love you, Delia, but I'm willing to wait. When the time is right, I'll merely have to think of another betrothal present."

He loved her. And he didn't seem to expect her to say it back right now. Did that make it all right to accept his gift?

Delia took a deep breath. "All right," she said, "as long as we're clear about that. How very kind and understanding you are to me." She opened her arms to him and stepped into his embrace.

Chapter Fourteen

Even though he had never attended services in the Llano Crossing Church, Jude felt a sense of coming home when he sat down in a middle pew with the Hestons. He watched the townspeople striding in in their Sunday best, smiling at each other—farmers, shop owners, laborers and their families—all of them God's children.

Even Charles Ladley, Jude supposed, as he caught sight of the mayor's son sitting proudly in the front pew next to Delia.

Yesterday, when Jude had spotted the exquisite thoroughbred mare outside Delia's house, he had guessed it was intended as a present for Delia—the beast might as well have had a big red satin bow around its neck. And what would induce Ladley to be giving Delia such a costly gift?

Delia had said Ladley didn't own her and had kissed Jude with every indication of sincerity and genuine feeling, but she and Ladley appeared very cozy together up front. Jude wondered if Ladley had been able to persuade Delia he was the better man. He hadn't thought

Delia so changeable, but he must have been wrong. His heart ached with a crushing sense of loss.

But You didn't bring me to church to spend my time envying Ladley, did You, Lord? Help me to concentrate on You, to hear what You have to say.

Jude resolutely wrenched his eyes and mind away from the couple. He opened his mouth to sing along with the rest of the congregation and felt a soothing peace descending upon him like a blessing. Even in the midst of the mayor's rambling attempt at a sermon, Jude knew he'd done right to come.

"All right, you spent a pretty penny on that nag," Mayor Ladley growled almost three weeks later. It was once again time for the Committee for Civic Improvement to meet, and as usual, the two Ladleys had come early so they could discuss things they didn't want Mrs. Ladley overhearing. "And why you didn't make the gift conditional on her agreeing to marry you, I don't understand—"

"Because I know that this way I'll get what I want more easily in the end," Charles Ladley told his father. He wasn't about to admit that Delia had told him she wasn't ready to consider his proposal any time soon and wouldn't accept the gift of the mare yet.

Ladley Senior harrumphed. "Time to move the project along, son. We need control of Delia Keller's money, and the only way that's going to happen is if you're her husband, not merely her adoring beau. What's next in the plan?"

The younger Charles took a sip of the rich port his father favored. He'd have preferred whiskey, but this stuff wasn't bad.

"Perhaps we'll go for a surprise moonlight picnic out at Ladley Hall one night, before it gets too cold. Very romantic, eh?" He winked. Calling Delia's new home "Ladley Hall" was a private joke between him and his father, a reference to when it—and Delia—would be firmly under his control.

"Capital, capital! To success then—" his father said with a wink and extended his glass to clink with his son's "—and control of the fortune. No woman should ever have control of that much money, eh? No long engagement. Appeal to her romantic notions, and get her to elope with you." He leaned closer to his son. "Compromise her, if you have to."

Charles was saved from the necessity of a reply by the door opening and their fellow committee members striding into the room.

"Ah, here are the fellows now," the mayor said, looking up as the others strode into the room. "Friends, why not be the first to congratulate my son, the future husband of Llano Crossing's own heiress? Of course, the news can't leave this room—he hasn't asked her yet."

The other men of the committee—Amos Dawson, Dixon Miller, Barton Jeffers, the mill owner, and Sheriff Jenkins—guffawed, pledged secrecy and slapped Charles on the back, calling him a sly dog.

Then Dawson, always the most impatient man on the committee, asked, "Does that mean we're about ready to seed the creek?" The phrase was a code for the plan shared only by the committee. "I'm tired of this one-horse town. I can't wait to be sippin' tequila on my *estancia* with a doe-eyed *señorita* fannin' my brow."

Ladley smirked at the banker's fantasy. "Dawson,

your patience is about to be rewarded. I think the time is nearly upon us. Miller, ready to play your role?"

"Yeah, I've been keepin' the entrance to that cave well-hidden—which ain't easy, as many hands as I've got workin' on my spread."

"Excellent, excellent," purred the mayor. "Of course, our biggest source of investment money will come from Miss Keller—assuming my son's suit is favored," he added, with a meaningful look at his son.

"Trust me, Father, it will be," Charles said, stroking his mustache. "She loves me a little more each day."

"And once he gets a ring on that gal's finger," Jeffers demanded, "what's to keep you Ladleys from just runnin' off to Mexico on your own? You'll have plenty of money then."

There was a chorus of agreement from the other two men.

"Why, I'm hurt you would think such a thing," the mayor said, looking it. "We have our honor as Southern gentlemen, so we would never dream of leaving you men holding the bag. Besides, there's greater money to be made if we're able to get all those gullible fools to invest. Never fear, gentlemen, we're in this to make as much money as possible."

"You have the gold in a safe place?" Dawson asked, still sounding suspicious.

"Of course," the mayor said.

In the last fortnight, Delia had seen Jude only at the site of her house. He was all business, and since the finishing process was at the stage where he needed help to complete the interior walls, he was always surrounded by men he'd hired to help him. The Jude who had kissed her so tenderly and smiled so winningly at her might never have existed.

Delia guessed Jude must have decided that because of the appearance of the horse, she had chosen Charles. She didn't want to let him continue in that mistaken notion, but all her efforts to speak to him alone had failed. She had tried going by the Hestons' house once in the evening, but Jude and his horse were gone, and she had spent a fruitless half hour chatting with the Hestons and pretending she'd just been out for a stroll.

She'd even thought of leaving him a note somewhere in the house where he'd be sure to find it, but finally, pride had taken over. Jude was apparently determined to believe what he wanted to believe, she decided, so she spent more time with Charles, who was never moody and prickly. She came to depend on his unfailing charm and ability to make her laugh. He always seemed to have a compliment at the ready, and every few days he came up with some small gift for her—a pair of onyx earbobs, a crystal vase to hold the flowers he picked from his mother's garden...

As for his mother, Jane Ladley had made it only too clear that she was delighted with her son's choice of sweetheart and couldn't wait to officially welcome her into the family. Her approval made up for the overheartiness of her husband, who nevertheless always seemed to be sizing up Delia—for what, she didn't know.

Charles kept telling her that he loved her. Could she love him? She enjoyed his gentle embraces that had never gone beyond what was proper between a courting couple. Was that enough? Many couples had less. They were now social equals, and he would fit into her world in every way—especially since Jude Tucker apparently didn't want to.

Shouldn't you pray about it? Now where had that thought come from? Delia glanced guiltily at the Bible sitting on her bedside table. She hadn't been reading it very much lately, as the dust that had settled on the worn, cracked leather cover attested.

"Señorita Keller, Mr. Charles says to tell you he will have to skip his ride with you this morning," the wizened old groom said when Delia arrived at the Ladley barn at their usual riding time. They'd ridden together almost every day, and Delia had become quite confident in her horsemanship.

Delia wrinkled her nose in disappointment. She was wearing a new dove-gray riding habit, which Miss Susan had finished for her only yesterday. It was among her first new garments of "half mourning" rather than full, solemn black.

"He said to tell you he was sorry, but he had to go to Mason on business," Manuel told her as he continued to curry her mare's gleaming black coat.

"That's fine, Manuel, but would you saddle up Zephyr anyway?" Delia asked.

The old groom's brow furrowed in uncertainty. "Señorita Keller, I do not know about thees.... You have not taken her out yet by yourself, *si?*"

"*Sí*—I mean, no, I haven't!" Delia gave him a sunny smile. "But thanks to Charles's expert teaching, I'm sure I'll have no problems. There has to be a first time, right? He'll be so proud of me! Don't worry, we won't go faster than a sedate trot, I promise."

Manuel still looked dubious, but at last he shrugged. "You should ride around town *solamente, sí?*"

"Only around town," Delia repeated, nodding. She would do that for the first little while, at least—and then she and the mare would head out of town. She'd give Zephyr her head, and they'd fly! The few times she and Charles had galloped their horses together, it had been delightful beyond words.

All went well while they remained in Llano Crossing. Delia felt the cynosure of all eyes as she rode the mare at a decorous walk down Main Street. She was so proud of the way the beautiful creature arched her lovely neck and picked her way delicately, as if she were walking on clouds.

Then all at once the mare shied at a puppy that came yipping out of an alleyway. Snorting, she gave a little half buck that nearly unseated Delia.

"Sorry, Miss Delia, didn't mean for Skippy to frighten your horse," Billy Dean, son of the mercantile owner, yelled, running out to scoop up his pup.

By that time Delia had succeeded in calming the mare somewhat with her voice. "No problem, Billy," she assured him, though the mare continued to sidle and curvet, her nostrils flared as she eyed the little dog as if fearing it might leap out of his young master's arms at her.

"Sure is a pretty hoss, Miss Delia."

There was nothing to this, Delia thought, as she bade Billy goodbye and rode on. She was ready to feel the wind in her face right now. She nudged the mare into a trot and headed her west. She would let the mare trot until they reached the site of her new house and see how the workmen were progressing, and then once she rode around the bend, she'd give Zephyr her head. That would show Jude Tucker how much she was pining for him!

When she arrived at the site, Jude, shirtsleeves rolled up, was directing two fellows who were carrying in a stack of fresh-cut two-by-fours. Shiloh was cropping grass in the shade of one of the big trees.

"How's it going, Mr. Tucker?" she called, being formal since there were a couple of laborers painting the outside of the house.

"Fine." Jude eyed her and the horse with hands on his hips, seemingly impatient at the interruption. "We'll be painting the walls by the end of the week. You'll be able to move in by Thanksgiving, as I promised."

"That's not so far away," she called, riding around in a circle because the echoing of hammers from within was making the mare more restive than before. "Are you sure?"

"Promised you, didn't I?" His gaze shifted to Zephyr, who was now sidling and pawing the ground. It was as if the mare had guessed her rider's intentions to let her run, and she was impatient to feel the wind in her mane. "Miss Delia, are you sure you're ready to be riding that horse without—by yourself?"

First he was curt, then he announced he doubted she could control the mare? She'd show him what a horsewoman she had become! "Perfectly sure," she informed him and nudged the mare with her heels.

"Delia, rein her in!" she heard Jude call after her, but she ignored him.

Chapter Fifteen

There was truly nothing to compare with the feeling of flying over the hard-packed clay road on the back of a fine horse. The wind had blown Delia's hat off half a mile or so back, and now her hair had come loose from its pins and was blowing loose behind her. The rolling mesquite-and cactus-dotted hills raced by.

Delia laughed aloud from the sheer joy of it. This was living! The only thing she could imagine being better would be to be riding astride rather than side-saddle. She knew it wasn't considered ladylike but perhaps if she did it only out here where it wasn't likely she'd be seen…

She'd ridden a mile beyond her house when the road grew rougher, and she decided she'd better rein in. It was then Delia realized she was in trouble, for Zephyr wasn't ready to slow down. Delia sat back in the saddle and pulled back on the reins, calling, "Whoa, girl. Easy, Zephyr."

Seizing the bit in her teeth, Zephyr lowered her head and galloped even faster. She'd been named for the wind, but a gentle western wind, not like this! Delia felt icy fingers of apprehension grip her—

Didn't she know she could fall off that horse and break her neck? He'd tried to warn her, and she'd ignored him, Jude told himself as Delia and the thoroughbred disappeared around the bend in a cloud of dust. *She had chosen to become Charles Ladley's problem, hadn't she?*

Does that give you an excuse not to do what's right? The Voice wasn't still or small at all this time.

"All right, Lord," he murmured, then cupped a hand around his mouth to call out to one of the painters. "Will, I'll be back in a few minutes." He ran over to where Shiloh was hobbled under one of the oak trees.

A minute later, he had vaulted onto the stallion's bare back and had kicked him into a gallop, gripping him with his knees and clutching a fistful of the buckskin's mane.

Please, Lord, let this worry be all for nothing. Let me find her cooling her mare down farther along the road, he prayed desperately as Shiloh's hooves devoured the road.

His hopes were dashed when he spied the black horse up ahead, riderless, blowing with her head down. Nearby lay a still, crumpled gray form.

"Delia!" He jumped his horse even as Shiloh skidded to a halt and ran to her.

She was unconscious but stirred slightly, moaning, as he touched her. There was a lump the size of a hen's egg already rising on her forehead, and a scrape where her cheek had collided with a stone. "Delia, you have to wake up!" he yelled down at her. *What if she never came to her senses again?*

Then he spied the canteen attached to her mare's saddle. *At least Ladley had taught her that much.* Wetting the handkerchief he yanked from his pocket, he bathed her forehead, all the while praying harder than he had ever prayed in his life.

Delia awoke to the feeling of a wet, cool cloth on her forehead and the trickling of water down the back of her neck. Wincing at the pain that lanced through her skull, she tried to open her eyes, only to be blinded by the sunlight shining directly into them. She tried to put a hand up to block the brilliant glare but felt a hand on her forearm, restraining her. She cried out in fear, struggling to rise to see who was keeping her down.

"Thank You, God," she heard Jude say. "Lie still, Delia. You've had a bad fall." He shifted himself so that he blocked the sunlight.

She lay still, squinting as she looked up into the pale eyes in that hard, angular face shadowed by his wide-brimmed hat. He ran his hands down her arms, probing.

"Do your arms hurt? Can you move them?" His tone was gentle and soothing, but his eyes hadn't yet lost their anxiety as he studied her.

"*Everything* hurts," she said, but flexed her fingers and bent her forearms experimentally. "I—I don't think anything's broken. Where's Zephyr?"

"What about your legs? Can you feel them? Can you move them? No, *don't try to get up,*" he said again. "Just tell me."

She knew she should remind him it wasn't proper to call them *legs* instead of *limbs* to a lady, but now wasn't the time to be prim. "Yes, I can feel everything," she said, wiggling them to demonstrate. "H-how did you know to come?"

"I tried to go back to work, but then I just *knew,*" he said simply. She saw Shiloh standing beyond him, saddleless. He'd been so worried, he hadn't even taken the time to saddle his horse. He'd ridden after her bareback.

"Where—where's Zephyr?" she asked, hardly bearing to hear the answer.

He moved again so she could see the mare for herself.

"A jackrabbit ran right out in front of us," Delia murmured. "It wasn't her fault."

"No, it wasn't," he agreed, but his eyes were compassionate as he said it. "Didn't you hear me call out to rein in? You could have been *killed,* Delia."

Again, his tone was gentle, but she could hear the barely relieved fear in his voice and closed her eyes against the stinging truth of his words. He was right; she knew it. She'd been foolhardy beyond all measure, and her willfulness could have cost her her life—or that of the beautiful mare.

"Do you think you can sit up?" Without waiting for permission, he slid one arm under her shoulder while the other cradled her neck and assisted her into a sitting position.

Every bone in her body felt bruised, and her lower back throbbed in tune with her throbbing head. Nausea churned in her stomach. *Don't let me be sick in front of this man, I beg of You.*

To distract herself, Delia looked back at her mare and saw now the way Zephyr stood so that her weight was shifted from the off foreleg. "Is her leg…*broken?*" she finally dared to ask. "Please—see if Zephyr's all right."

Jude got to his feet and strode over to the mare. Zephyr raised her lovely head as he approached, but she stood still, trembling, as he took hold of her trailing reins and ran a hand gently over her legs. Delia saw her flinch as his hand reached her off foreleg. Straightening, he spoke softly to the mare, leading her to take a few steps.

Delia saw the horse dip her head every time she put weight on the off foreleg. Jude tied her reins to a nearby mesquite before turning back to her.

"Nothing's broken, but she's lame."

"She'll recover?"

He nodded. "After a while. She'll have to be on stall rest until her leg heals. I'll take you home on Shiloh, and lead her. Maybe the doc should check you over."

"That's not necessary—" Delia began, but he was already lifting her to her feet by scooping one hand under her backside while keeping the other around her shoulders.

As soon as she put her weight on her left foot, however, pain zinged up her leg and she sagged against Jude, stifling a cry.

"Looks like that mare's not the only one who's lame," he said, and before she knew what he was about, he had picked her up and was carrying her toward his stallion.

"You'll have to ride astride," he told her, "and hold on to Shiloh's mane. He'll just follow me." He boosted her onto the silver buckskin's back as if she weighed nothing.

Delia felt her face flame scarlet as she looked down at the length of stockinged leg and lacy petticoat showing above her short riding boots. But Jude, leading the mare slowly beside his stallion, either didn't notice, was unmoved by the sight or perhaps was saving his energy for the long trek back to town.

When they reached her house, Delia kept her head down, embarrassed, as Jude informed the workmen who came to see them that he'd be back as soon as he had her situated at home and the mare back in the Ladley stable.

"You p-poor d-dear!" Miss Susan cried sympathetically, red-faced and panting as she ran into the house minutes after Jude had left. "Mr. Tucker stopped at the shop to tell me what had happened, and he looked so worried I thought I'd better leave the shop early. Does it hurt very badly?" she asked, pointing to the leg Delia had propped on another chair, with a cold cloth wrapped around it.

"You didn't have to do that," Delia said, but in truth she was glad to see her. "It's sprained, Jude says. I deserve every ache I've got and worse. I know I could have killed that horse."

"Don't be so hard on yourself, honey," Miss Susan said sympathetically. "You're going to mend—and so will the mare, Mr. Tucker said. We'll wrap your ankle, and I'll fix you some willowbark tea that'll help the pain. You've got a lump on your forehead and a scraped cheek, too, did you know? And didn't I see your grandpa's cane under my bed? You'll be needing that for a while."

"I'd forgotten it was there," Delia murmured, but she was thinking about what Jude had said before he'd left—

"Delia, I know you love that horse, and it's true she's

a beauty, but please, if you've ever believed me about anything, ask Ladley to get you a horse that's less high-strung."

"She's not my horse, Jude," she had told him. "He tried to give her to me, it's true, but I told him I couldn't accept such a gift. I—I'll tell him I'm not ready for her yet—maybe ever."

He gave her an astonished look. "Then she wasn't a—a betrothal present? You're not engaged to wed Ladley?"

"No." She saw him start at her answer. "I told you it was too soon to commit myself to Charles—or anyone, for that matter. A beautiful horse didn't change that."

He blinked, and suddenly his features relaxed and he looked almost happy. "All right then. I—I reckon that's good. I'll just take your—the—mare on to the Ladley stable and check on you later."

Chapter Sixteen

"Delia, sweetheart, I came as soon as I heard...."
Charles rushed past Miss Susan, into the parlor and
over to where Delia sat with her foot propped up on an
adjoining chair. He glanced outside, where dusk was
drawing in. "I'm sorry, my business took longer than
I'd thought it would. I arrived home minutes ago, and
Mother told me what happened. Are you in pain, my
dear? Why, that bruise, and that scrape on your face!
And your poor ankle. That blasted nag!"

She'd been half-afraid he would be angry—justifi-
ably—with her for laming the valuable horse, but he
was only concerned for her. "Charles, I'm *all right,*"
Delia said, trying to stop his flow of regret. "My ankle's only sprained, and these will fade in a few days,"
she added, pointing to the wounds on her face. "It's not
the horse's fault, it's mine, as Jude Tucker told me when
he found me. He was right—I shouldn't have been out
galloping alone. Thank God nothing worse happened.
I'd never forgive myself if Zephyr had broken a leg."

"Delia, I'm much more concerned about your safety
than about a horse or anything in this world," he told

her. His voice was a caress in itself. "Tucker will be rewarded for assisting you. He wasn't too stern with you, was he? I'd have to thrash him if he was!" He was almost jovial now.

"No, of course not. I—I think perhaps Zephyr's too much horse for me."

Charles moved to cup her cheek in his hand, seemingly oblivious of Miss Susan standing by the door. "Nonsense, darling," he reassured her. "We'll have some more lessons, and by the end of them, you'll be riding like a cavalryman, I promise you! Just think, we're both using canes now, although thankfully yours is only temporary.

"It's too bad this happened," Charles went on. "I'd thought to take you on a picnic tonight, out at your future house, the weather continuing so mild for fall."

"That is too bad," Delia agreed. "I would have enjoyed that. Perhaps we can do that another—"

"Ah, but we can still have a picnic of sorts, though in your yard here, not out there," Charles interrupted. "Cook had already packed it for us, and it's sitting out in the landau. There's no sense in wasting it because of a sprained ankle. I'll set everything up on the grass, and then I have only to help you outside."

Delia's eyes met Miss Susan's as he made his way back outside.

"He expects you to hobble outside, just so he can call it a picnic?" Miss Susan groused. "Plumb foolishness, I say."

Inwardly, Delia also wished they could eat at her table so she wouldn't have to make an additional painful effort of negotiating the steps, but she didn't want to spoil Charles's attempt to provide a romantic evening. But she felt awkward about going outside to eat with Charles, leaving Miss Susan inside by herself—as if she were a servant and not a guest in her house.

"Everything's ready," Charles proclaimed, returning inside. "Here's your shawl, in case it gets chilly, and your cane, Delia. You can lean on my arm."

"Miss Susan, join us, please," Delia said.

"Oh, no, I wouldn't dream of intruding on your picnic—"

"And we wouldn't dream of leaving you out, would we, Charles?" she said, meeting his eyes.

Delia thought she saw a flash of frustration streak across Ladley's handsome, agreeable face before he chimed in, "No, of course not. There's plenty of food. If we could merely borrow a table service from your kitchen, Delia, since Cook didn't know we'd have anyone joining us…"

"Thank you both—it's very kind of you—but I'm not hungry," Miss Susan said. "You two go ahead and enjoy it. Please, Delia."

Delia watched her go, aware of Charles's almost palpable relief that it would be only the two of them. She sighed and decided she had done her best. She might as well enjoy the meal Charles had brought.

Once she had made her way outside with some difficulty to the "picnic spot" in her front yard, and was assisted to sit at the edge of the linen cloth Charles had spread out, Delia sighed with pleasure and discovered she was hungry. Maisie, the Ladleys' cook, had indeed outdone herself. There were roasted quail, new potatoes, green beans almondine, chocolate cake and a large jar of cold tea, with delicate cut-glass tumblers set in front of heirloom china. Charles had even brought a pair of candelabras, which he lit with great ceremony.

The food was as delicious as it looked. But Charles was abnormally quiet, his words stilted when he did speak. Delia wondered what was troubling him. Was he merely disappointed that they couldn't be having this picnic out at her house site?

"What a lot of trouble Maisie went to, Charles," Delia said. "Please thank her for me. It was thoughtful of you to think of this, too. I'm so sorry to have ruined it by going and getting myself injured as I did."

"Not at all, Delia. I had hoped this evening… But there'll be another time. I guess I just have a lot on my mind. Forgive me for being poor company." There was an uncharacteristic strain to his mouth.

Delia wondered what he had begun to say about his hopes for this evening. Surely after their talk the other day, he hadn't been going to propose under the moonlight this evening or try to push their relationship further than she was ready for it to go? Perhaps her injury had really been a blessing in disguise.

"Heard some news in town today," Lucy Heston said from across the table as she passed her husband a plate of corn fritters with one hand, while handing Jude a bowl of buttered biscuits with the other.

"Oh? What's that?" James Heston asked. "Don't tell me, Llano Crossing's going to become the new state capital instead of Austin, and Mayor Ladley's running for governor."

"No, silly," Lucy Heston said, giving her spouse a loving but exasperated look. "The mayor's calling a big meeting to be held next Sunday night, and he wants everyone there."

"Humph," he snorted. "Wonder what he's up to? No good, probably."

"Now, Jim," his wife reproved him in her gentle way, "you don't know that."

"Maybe not, but speaking of Mayor Ladley, while you were out gallivantin'—" he winked at his wife to show he was joking "—he paid me a call and asked me to read the Scripture at church come Sunday. He says he's tryin' t' share the responsibilities a' leadin' the worship service," Heston explained, but he looked skeptical. "Huh! If ya ask me, he'd do better to go beat the bushes an' find us a new preacher."

"Maybe that's what he's going to announce at this Sunday-night meeting," Jude suggested.

"No, they say it's got nothing to do with church, rather some plan the Committee for Civic Improvement has developed."

"Guess we'll have t' wait and see."

"What passage are you supposed to read?" Jude asked.

"The part about the Good Samaritan. Jude, I kin read, I reckon," Heston said, "but I'm all slow and stumbly when I have t' read out loud. It's you who should be doin' it—you have a fine reading voice."

Jude shook his head, wishing now he hadn't read to the old couple out of the Psalms a few times in the evenings, but the Hestons read the Bible every evening after dinner, and when he was around, he'd taken part. "I'm just a carpenter. And besides, he didn't ask me." He wanted to help the kindly old man who'd become his friend, however. "Why don't you come out to the barn, and you can practice reading the passage in front of me?"

Mr. Heston reluctantly admitted that might work.

Five days had passed, and Delia found that Miss Susan had given good advice about her ankle. By wrapping it firmly in linen strips, keeping her foot propped up on a cushion and staying off of it as much as possible, using her cane and drinking willowbark tea three times a day, the ankle had gotten progressively less painful and swollen.

The high point of her day was when Jude stopped by at sunset every day on his way home from the worksite, ostensibly to report on his progress and ask how her injuries were healing, but he stayed and chatted with both Delia and Miss Susan. He always asked the latter if Donley Morrison had bothered her any further, and the seamstress always replied in the negative. Once, Jude even took supper with them, since he had finished late that evening, and they were just sitting down to eat when he arrived.

Miss Susan seemed to always have an excuse to leave them alone during part or all of his visit, but while Jude seemed in no great hurry to leave, neither did he say or do anything that indicated any wish to deepen their friendship. He seemed as if he was waiting for something, but what?

Mystified, she'd mentioned it to Miss Susan one night after Jude left. "Maybe he's waiting for you to make up your mind about Ladley," the older woman said tartly.

Delia sighed. If she was honest with herself, she already had. She valued Charles's friendship, and didn't want to hurt him, but she had nothing in common with him but social position—certainly not enough on which to base a marriage. She loved Jude, she knew that now. But for all she knew, he was still planning to return to Nevada once her house was built.

Show me what to do, Lord, she prayed each night.

Now it was Sunday morning, and as Delia waited on the porch for Charles to stop by in his carriage, she found she was able to put weight on her ankle without too much discomfort. She'd keep the cane with her for now, though, just in case.

Jude sat with the Hestons in their usual pew in the little church and did his best not to stare at Delia sitting up front next to the mayor's son. Perhaps while they waited for the service to start, he ought to say a little prayer for his boss that his reading would go smoothly. Oddly enough, Heston didn't seem nervous about it anymore, but surely a little prayer wouldn't hurt.

Three hymns were sung, as was the usual pattern. Then, instead of the mayor leaving the front pew and heading to the lectern, he kept his seat and his son got up.

"I have an announcement before Mr. Heston reads the Bible passage. My father asked me to inform you that along with a bit of a sore throat, he seems to have lost his voice this morning and can't speak above a whisper. He's hoping to be able to lead the meeting tonight if he rests his voice, but if not, I will take his place. So once the Scripture is read…why, I suppose we can all just sing another hymn and go home to our Sunday dinners a bit early," he concluded with a genial laugh.

"Couldn't you read his sermon notes?" an old man in the crowd asked.

Charles gave a self-deprecating smile of regret. "I'd be happy to, but being the gifted speaker that my father is, he always speaks extemporaneously. He never makes any notes."

There was a murmuring among the congregation, and Jude saw Mr. Heston and his wife exchange a look.

"Mr. Heston," Charles said, beckoning to the open Bible on the lectern.

James Heston stood, smoothing the frock coat he only wore on Sundays, then reached into his breast pocket. "Soon as I get my spectacles…" He began to look worried, then patted both trouser pockets. His weathered, gnarled hands dived into them and came up empty.

"Lucy," he said, looking down at his wife, "do you by any chance have my spectacles?"

She looked back at him, bewildered. "No, Jim, of course I don't have them. Didn't you bring them?"

He clapped a hand to his forehead. "Oh no!" he exclaimed. "I must have left them on the bedside table, after goin' over the passage this very mornin'! Folks, I'm sorry, but I don't have it memorized, so I can't read this mornin'."

Was it Jude's imagination or was Heston avoiding his eyes? There was something almost *practiced* about his distress.

Charles Ladley looked nonplussed. "I suppose I—"

"But Jude Tucker, here, can read it," Mr. Heston interrupted quickly.

Jude shot a look at the wily old man, sure now that

he'd been set up. He thought about refusing, but then Jude saw that Delia had turned around and was staring at him, her eyes wide at this surprising turn of events.

Chapter Seventeen

Ladley began to demur, saying, "Oh, but I could certainly…"

Go read the story, Jude.

Jude rose and made his way to the pulpit, aware that members of the congregation were whispering and poking one another. Both Mr. and Mrs. Heston were grinning.

Jude walked up to the pulpit on shaky legs. He found the Bible already open to the correct place. "Our reading this morning is in Luke, chapter ten," he began, looking out over the sea of faces. It had been so long since he'd done anything like this. *Help me, Lord, if You want me to do this.* "A certain man went down from Jerusalem to Jericho, and fell among thieves.…"

His voice started out unsure, like a key being inserted in a lock that was rusty from disuse. He stumbled over a word or two. Then Jude felt peace sweeping over him—and certainty—and by the time he reached the part about the Samaritan finding the wounded man and taking him to the inn to recover, his voice was ring-ing with confidence. When he finished the passage, *"amens"* were popping up all over the congregation.

He closed the Bible with a soft thump and started to step away from the pulpit, but now Mr. Heston spoke up. "That was right fine, Jude! Why don't you expound on that a little, tell us what you think it ought t' mean to us?"

"Oh, no, I don't think—" Jude started to say, just as the younger Ladley said, "Mr. Heston, surely we oughtn't to put Mr. Tucker on the spot...."

"Yeah, why don't you say a few words?" Mrs. Dean, wife of the mercantile owner, called out. "Man who reads th' Bible as nice as that prob'ly has some thoughts to go with it!"

There was an answering chorus of agreement, though Mayor Ladley sat there looking uncomfortable, as if he'd just swallowed a horny toad.

But it was the surprise of seeing Delia's green eyes, sympathetic and encouraging, and the swift nod she gave him that made Jude believe he could do as they were asking and *should* do it. He sent up another quick prayer that he be given the right words to say.

"And occasionally," he concluded some twenty minutes later, "we need to look beneath the surface to see that someone is hurting and not assume that it's someone else's role to help him. Do as the Samaritan did."

He looked up from the Bible and saw the Hestons beaming at him like proud parents and Delia, as well as the rest of the congregation, looking thoughtful.

"I...I reckon that's all that needs to be said about the Good Samaritan, at least by me this morning," Jude concluded, humbled at what had just taken place. It was as if he had never left his little church in Tennessee, as if those war years, and all the wrong things he had done during them, were wiped away. "Why don't we sing another hymn like Mr. Ladley said, and then perhaps Mr. Heston would like to give the final blessing." He grinned triumphantly at James Heston, who accepted Jude's getting the last laugh with good grace and managed to do a fine job.

Afterward, it seemed to Jude as if he was the center of a whirlwind. Most of the congregation came up and shook his hand and complimented him on the fine little sermon he'd done with no prior notice. Several asked him if he'd ever thought about becoming a preacher, and a few even urged him to consider becoming the pastor of this church, even though as far as they knew he'd never been to seminary.

"You did a fine job. I knew you could do it," Delia praised him, when it came to her turn to shake his hand on the way out. Ladley, right behind her, nodded curtly at him and muttered something that might have been approval. Delia looked as if she wanted to say something more, but then Charles touched her elbow, reminding her they were to have Sunday dinner with his parents, and steered her on.

Jude, turning to greet the next person who wanted to shake his hand, missed the rebellious set to Delia's mouth after Ladley's high-handedness.

"You sure did yourself proud, son," Heston told him on the way out of the church, and his wife murmured her agreement. "You've been a preacher before, haven't you?" It was a statement, not a question.

Jude frowned at Heston, putting his finger over his mouth, hoping no one among the stragglers had overheard Heston. "Thanks, but let's talk about it later."

Heston nodded. "Mum's the word."

"Delia Keller sure looked lovely today," Mrs. Heston said, and looked meaningfully at Jude.

"She'd look a lot better standin' next to Jude than with that polecat Charles Ladley," growled Heston, before Jude could form an answer. "Don't think I didn't notice how often you glanced her way," he said to Jude.

What was he supposed to say to that? Was he supposed to admit that he lay awake every night, thinking of her, wondering why her eyes said she cared about him whenever he came to see her, but around town, he kept seeing her with Ladley?

Delia knew as little as anyone else in Llano Crossing about the subject of the meeting that evening. She only knew Charles was like a coiled spring, filled with a suppressed excitement that caused his eyes to dance with the secret they held. His father seemed possessed by the same energy, and at the Sunday dinner table, while she and Mrs. Ladley had talked about her new house, Delia saw father and son exchange looks that seemed charged with meaning.

"Thank you all for coming," Mayor Ladley said, still hoarse, but managing to get the words out as he arose from his chair in the front of the church. Alongside him sat his son, Amos Dawson, Dixon Miller, Sheriff Jenkins and Barton Jeffers. "I know all of you have been wondering about the subject of this meeting. We will keep you waiting no longer."

Miss Susan, sitting next to Delia, said in a stage whisper, "It's about time!" and everyone chuckled—even the mayor, who said, "Yes, it *is* about time. About time Llano Crossing's citizens begin to enjoy the prosperity they so richly deserve, a prosperity that was beginning to dawn until the War Between the States robbed us of the flower of our youth, left many others grievously wounded—" Ladley paused to glance meaningfully at his son behind him "—and beset many of us with ruinous taxes."

"You ain't plannin' on us secedin' from the Union, are ya?" called a man in the crowd who had lost an arm in the war. "'Cause I've already done that once, and once was enough."

The mayor smiled again and made a gesture for quiet. "Never fear, fellow citizens of Llano Crossing. As your duly elected mayor, as much as I would have liked to see our boys in gray prevail, I would not countenance anything so foolish as a new rebellion. No, what the Committee for Civic Improvement had in mind was a way of bringing prosperity to our town and its citizens, and our town only."

He paused, until it was so quiet Delia could have heard a pin drop in the little church, then cleared his throat. "Several months ago, our own Miss Delia Keller—" the mayor gestured toward her "—was the recipient of a windfall, which has transformed her life. I am telling you now that all of you who participate will also be receiving a financial bounty that will transform yours."

A buzz of excitement rose from the pews. The mayor tolerated it for a moment before lifting a hand for silence.

"Before I ask Dixon Miller to come forward and announce the plan, I am going to have to ask that everyone present pledge themselves to maintaining secrecy. This plan will not succeed if rumors start flying and others not of our town start flocking in to take the hard-won riches that the committee seeks to share with all of you good citizens of Llano Crossing."

Mayor Ladley's eyes roved over the attendees. "I cannot stress the need for discretion enough, good citizens. I am going to ask those of you who are able to commit a sum of money. I want to assure those who feel they do not have any spare cash that they need not despair, for a role can be found for you, too. A rising tide floats all boats, does it not? You need not indicate how much you will invest at this time. That is a matter for reflection and discussion at home and, of course, prayer," he added unctuously. "Do I have your solemn promises of secrecy? All those willing, stand now and raise your right hands to pledge your commitment. All those who feel they cannot so pledge, please leave now."

Everyone stood, glancing at each other, wondering what the plan was. No one left.

"Please repeat after me—"

The attendees dutifully stood and repeated phrase by phrase as the mayor rasped it out, pledging support of the plan and utmost secrecy, with a penalty of having to leave the county if they should break faith. Neighbors exchanged uneasy glances but completed the pledge, eager to hear what was going to make them rich.

Delia had stood with the rest, but she had not raised her hand nor repeated the words. No one seemed to notice. She couldn't help wondering what her grandpa would have thought of all this or, for that matter, what Jude Tucker was thinking. She had seen him sitting with the Hestons in their usual place when she'd come in with Charles.

The mayor clasped his large, meaty hands together

and beamed at everyone. "Congratulations on your willingness to enter into this adventure with us. I had hoped you would, and I have not been disappointed. I knew I could trust all of you. Dixon Miller, will you please come now and explain the plan?"

There was a renewed hum of talk as the rancher stepped forward. "Some of you may know," he said, "that there is a small, spring-fed creek on my land that waters my southeast pasture before emptying into the Llano River. Not long ago, one of my ranch hands, Donley Morrison, was watering his horse at this creek when he spotted something in the water that made his heart beat quite a bit faster. Donley, come up here and show the folks what you found."

From the back of the room, the barrel-chested man Delia hadn't seen since that day in Miss Susan's shop ambled forward, grinning self-consciously. Delia felt Miss Susan move closer to her.

Donley faced the audience, reaching into the pocket of his worn, patched trousers. He raised his clenched fist and then opened it, palm upward, to reveal an irregular lump about the size of a robin's egg.

Even from where she sat, Delia knew she was looking at gold. The townspeople gasped as one.

"Yes, it's gold," Miller said, "discovered in my creek. But I care about this town, so I'm not seeking to keep the profit to myself, surprising as that may be. After Donley made this discovery, I followed that creek to its source in a little cavern, a cavern that's so well-hidden I had never suspected its presence. You wouldn't find it, either, unless I showed you. This cave's only big enough for a couple a' men to stoop over in it, but there's tiny passageways leadin' off from that that're only big enough for a wiry feller to crawl into. He tells me there's veins a' gold so rich in this cave that you can't begin t' imagine the wealth to be had if we could just get to 'em. And that, my dear fellow citizens of Llano Crossing, is where you come in. Mr. Jeffers, would you mind explainin' the rest?"

Barton Jeffers, a big, imposing man with jowly, florid cheeks, stepped forward as Dixon Miller took his seat.

"What we're proposing is an association, I suppose you could call it. Obviously, money will be needed to pay for development of the mine—enlarging those narrow passages, paying miners to dig it out, and so forth. There would be various levels of membership, in accordance with how much investment money you're willing and able to put in. And your profits would be reaped accordingly."

"So the more money you put in, the more you make?" a man in the back called out.

Jeffers smiled like a teacher pleased at his class. "Exactly. But everyone who puts in anything will see a handsome return. What we in the committee envision is a way to keep the profits within the community, rather than having gold-hungry prospectors pouring into Llano Crossing and turning it into a boomtown, with all the accompanying evils that go with it—more saloons, gamblers, unsavory women… With the profits from the mine, our prosperity will, in turn, attract quality settlers who value a safe, civilized community."

"Sounds good to me," someone called out from behind Delia. "Where do I sign?"

Jeffers held up a hand. "I appreciate your eagerness, but as Mayor Ladley said, we want y'all to think about the plan, discuss within your families how much you feel able to contribute. Come back here Wednesday night, prepared to commit yourselves wholeheartedly, if you agree. Meanwhile, remember you've pledged yourselves to secrecy. If you should happen to encounter anyone from outside Llano Crossing, you cannot speak of this plan. And now I think it's time to end this meeting. Mayor Ladley, will you dismiss us in prayer?"

Chapter Eighteen

After the meeting, Charles, Delia and Miss Susan drove back to the parsonage, but when Delia would have followed the seamstress inside, Charles put a hand on her wrist.

"Why don't we go for a drive, Delia? It's a nice night, and I'd like to hear what you thought of the sche—the plan."

She hesitated. "Could we just sit in the parlor and talk for a while, Charles? I—I'm a little tired, but I *do* want to discuss what they said."

His mouth drooped sulkily. "I suppose," he said with a heavy sigh, "though I must confess I liked it better before *that spinster* came to live with you. I feel as if we have no privacy with her in there." He nodded toward the house. "She's probably always got her ear to the keyhole. She isn't planning to live with you forever, is she?"

Delia stared at him, surprised and annoyed at the peevish tone she'd never heard him use before. "Miss Susan," she said carefully, "would never *dream* of listening at keyholes, and she's welcome in my house for as long as she cares to stay."

"I'm sorry," Charles said hastily, taking hold of her hand. "I suppose I'm a little fatigued myself, after working with the committee for so long to bring this plan to the town. Friends again?"

Delia nodded, still inwardly uneasy. She had just seen a side of Charles he'd never shown before, and coupled with her earlier misgivings about committing herself to him and her growing love for Jude Tucker— no matter what his feelings were for her—made her more sure than ever that she needed to make a clean break with Charles Ladley.

"Don't you think the plan is marvelous, Delia?" he said, as they settled themselves on the horsehair couch. "Just think, you and I'll be among the primary shareholders. We'll be richer than the proverbial Croesus!" Even in the flickering lamplight, his eyes gleamed and his grin was exuberant—amazing, since he had been so petulant only minutes ago.

"Primary shareholders?" she echoed. "You have money to invest?"

"Some, though not as much as you, of course," he admitted. His eyes had left hers and seemed to focus on a point across the room. "But, darling, one of these days I'll be your husband. What's yours becomes ours, right? Just as what's mine becomes yours," he added quickly, glancing at her. "We can use the money to make more money—that's the way it's done."

"I…I see." Delia pulled her shawl closer around her, as if the October evening chill had penetrated the cozy little house. She hadn't thought about it much before tonight, but whoever she married would be the one who

had the final say in how her money—*their money*—
would be spent. Charles, she sensed now, would always
assume that as the man his opinion was the only one
that mattered in how the money was spent, no matter
where the money had come from.

"Don't look so worried, sweetheart," Charles said,
slipping his arm around her shoulders to pull her close.
"Ah, Delia, that's what I love about you. In your heart,
you're still a poor preacher's granddaughter, and even
now, the idea of fabulous wealth still makes you a bit
nervous, doesn't it? Don't ever change, darling. Stay as
innocent and sweet as you are."

Delia turned toward him just as he leaned closer to
kiss her cheek. She pulled hastily away.

He pulled away and studied her. "I-is something
wrong?"

"I—I…" She didn't want to say the words that would
hurt him, but she must. "I guess it's true that talking
about vast sums of money makes me nervous," she
agreed.

"I understand, sweetheart. How much were you
thinking of contributing? Maybe just saying it aloud
to me will make it easier to get used to the idea."

She swallowed hard. "A thousand dollars…"

Charles's jaw dropped. "A thousand dollars? *That's
all?* Delia, I thought you supported the committee's
plan! A thousand dollars from one with a fortune such
as yours is…well, it's paltry."

Oh, dear, she had offended him after all, and that
would make the other matter she had to discuss that
much harder to broach.

"Charles, I am willing to support the project, but
think about it—*I* don't need the money the mine would

make, do I? I already have more than enough—I don't want to be greedy."

Charles's lips compressed to a tight, bloodless line. For a long moment he said nothing, and then he let out a breath and his features relaxed again. "Of course, you're right. I had forgotten how generous and unselfish you are. You want the people who have not experienced your good luck to enjoy the profits."

As she had thought so often, Delia wanted to say that she'd rather have her father back than all the luck in the world, but she thought better of it. "Something like that, yes. It's good of you to understand."

"I love you, Delia. Why wouldn't I?" he said. "All right, a thousand it is." He started to rise. "Maybe I should go. It's been a long day."

Don't love me, she thought. *That will make this so much harder.*

"There's more I need to say, Charles," Delia said and watched as he sank back onto the couch, his confidence faltering now.

"I've valued—that is, I *value* our friendship, Charles," she said. "I always will, and I hope you will do the same. But..." *Help me, Lord.* "I can see you want it to become something more than that. I thought I just wasn't ready, but it's become more and more clear to me that...that I don't think you—that is, *we*—are right for each other. We value different things," she said, her eyes stinging as she saw his eyes widen with pain. "No matter how used I grow to my new wealth, I think I will always be, deep down, the preacher's poor granddaughter, a—a church mouse."

"Don't say that, Delia, don't!" he cried, and then astonished her by kneeling at her feet and taking both her hands in his while he stared up at her, his eyes plead-ing. "Don't tell me you can never love me!"

Her stomach clenched with compassion as she saw a tear snake its way down his suddenly pale cheek. She hated hurting him.

"I *do* love you—as a friend, Charles. I'll always be that, as I said. You—and your family—have been very kind to me. But I can't love you as a wife should, I know that now. I...I also know the right woman is out there for you."

"The right woman for me is *you,* Delia," he in-sisted. "Please, think about what you're doing! How can I te—" He broke off, and once again Delia was left wondering what he'd been about to say.

She stood up, letting her hands slip from his. "I *have* thought about it, Charles—believe me, I have."

"Is there...is there someone else, Delia? Has that Jude Tucker been making you promises, telling you lies about me?" He stood up, and now his eyes glittered with something that made Delia cold all over.

She had to set him straight. "No, Charles. We don't talk about you. Mr. Tucker is building a house for me, and mostly that's what we speak of. I'd better say good-night now, Charles. Please remember I'd like to con-tinue being your friend, if you're willing."

"We'll always be friends, of course," he said stiffly, but he did not meet her eyes.

"See, Jude, you won't even have to go back to Ne-vada to be a miner again," Heston groused, once they had returned home from the meeting at the church. "I suppose after you finish Miss Delia's house, you'll sign on with the committee as soon as it starts hirin'."

Jude turned to his boss. "It might be a good idea."

Heston snorted. "What d'ya mean by that?"

"It might be wise to keep an eye on what they're doing."

"So *you* think there's a fox in the chicken coop, too!" Heston exclaimed, slapping his knee. "Dadgum it, but I knew you were smart, son! You think these old boys're up t' something like I do, don't you?"

"I don't know," Jude said thoughtfully, rubbing his thumb and forefinger over his chin. "But there's never been any gold found anywhere in these parts before, has there?"

"Not so much as a glimmer," Mrs. Heston supplied from her rocking chair, and Heston nodded in confirmation.

"It's *possible* that Morrison really found gold," Jude pointed out.

Heston gave a skeptical snort again. "I wouldn't trust him far's I could throw him, any more than I do his boss. I'm pretty sure that's the same fella that fired a shot and spooked my gelding that evenin' we met, Jude. That cave he's talkin' about used to be on my property. I had to go down into it once to rescue a calf that fell in there, but I can't say I looked around much—too busy keepin' that bawlin' calf on my shoulders and climbin' back out at the same time."

Jude was thoughtful for a minute. "Have you ever heard of pyrite, Jim? Fool's gold?" Jude asked. "Looks just like the real thing."

"But it ain't. You think that's what it is?"

"'All that glitters isn't gold,'" Mrs. Heston quoted, picking up her crocheting.

Jude shrugged. "I sure couldn't tell from a glimpse

of that nugget so far from me. It would take an assayer to say for sure. Now, pyrite's not always a bad thing. Sometimes it's mixed up with copper or iron."

"But it ain't valuable as gold, is it?"

Jude shook his head. "And we only have Morrison's—and the committee's—word that what he was showing us was really found where he said it was." *A man who'd beat his wife might do anything else, especially if he was paid enough.*

Heston gave a low whistle. "Jude, you're smart as a tree full a' owls, you know that? So you're plannin' to hire on t' see what they've found?"

"Thought I might, for a spell. I promised Delia I'd be done with her house by Thanksgiving, and there's not much for me to do outside with winter coming on, anyway. I heard someone say they're planning to start hiring in November, though they don't plan to start working in the mine till the end of winter. Once they've enlarged those passages, though, it shouldn't take long for me to figure out if it's the real thing. Were you planning to invest?"

Heston gave a bark of laughter. "Even if I *had* a passel a' greenbacks, which I don't, I wouldn't put 'em into anything Dixon Miller or the mayor're involved in."

Jude grinned. "You might be passing up your chance to be rich, Jim."

"I'm already rich, boy, in the things that matter. Got me a good wife," he said, jerking his head toward Mrs. Heston, "got some good land, my health, a good relationship with the good Lord. And good friends." He nodded at Jude. "What else does a man need?"

"Well said," Jude murmured. Silence fell over the three, and Jude found his thoughts straying to Delia.

He'd caught glimpses of her lovely profile as she listened to the committee's plan, and there hadn't been the avid excitement there that he'd seen on the faces of many of the other townspeople. Perhaps it was because she already had plenty of money, but Jude had thought she'd seemed troubled rather than detached.

Chapter Nineteen

"You look a mite wilted," Miss Susan said the next morning as she and Delia washed and dried their breakfast dishes. "Did you get any sleep last night?"

"Not much," Delia admitted, wondering if the older woman guessed why. Her eyes felt heavy and her brain foggy, but she was also aware of a dawning sense of relief.

"Stop me if you don't want me meddlin', but I could hear Charles's voice raised through my door last night. Couldn't tell what he was saying, but he sounded upset."

"He was," Delia said. "I'm not willing to contribute enough money to the committee's project to suit him."

"Good for you for havin' backbone! Don't you let him sweet-talk you into changin' your mind, either."

"Oh, I don't think he'll be doing any more of that," Delia said, then told her the rest of what she had said to Charles.

Miss Susan dropped her dish towel and clapped her hands. "Delia, that's the best news I've heard in a year of Sundays! I never, ever thought Charles Ladley was worthy of you. Well, I'll make myself scarce when Jude stops by tonight after work so you can tell him."

Delia's hands stilled in the soapy water and she stared at Miss Susan. "You think I should *throw* myself at him? I couldn't do that!"

"Why ever not? Don't you love him?"

The question caught Delia off guard. She'd never said it aloud before. "Yes," she whispered; then, "Yes, but what if he rejects me again—what if he tells me again he's going back to Nevada as soon as possible?"

"What if he *doesn't?*" Miss Susan countered. "All I'm saying is, tell him what you just told me, and unless I miss my guess, he'll be happy to take it from there."

Delia found she couldn't stop the smile from spreading across her face. She felt like dancing for joy, even with her still-touchy ankle. "One way to find out," she said. "Oh, how I *wish* I had a horse—I'd go out there this morning!"

The thought reminded her of Zephyr and made her wistful, in spite of her happiness. She hoped the affectionate, spirited mare was recovering from her lameness. Charles would probably sell her, and she'd never see her again.

"That's the spirit," Miss Susan approved, hanging up her dish towel. "Well, I'd better get to the shop."

"I'll walk with you," Delia said. After her fall from the horse, she hadn't been escorting Miss Susan to work because of her sprained ankle, but after intercepting the glare Donley Morrison had sent Miss Susan's way when he'd been standing in the front of the church last night, Delia thought she'd better resume doing it.

"There's no need," Miss Susan tried to tell her. "If

Donley was going to do something, I think he'd have
done it by now—"

Delia wasn't convinced, after seeing the expression
in the big cowboy's eyes last night. Grabbing her cane,
she followed her out the door. "It's no trouble. Doc
Jones told me I needed to start using my ankle again,
a little at a time."

They were halfway to the shop when Miss Susan
suddenly said, "Delia, be careful about Charles."

Delia paused in midstride. "What are you saying?
Charles may be disappointed about us, but I know he'd
never hurt me."

"It's just a feeling I have, Delia. I don't think anyone
really *knows* Charles. And I can tell you this now—you
didn't know Charles spent a good deal of time above
the saloon, did you? You understand what I'm saying?"

"How do you know this?" *Charles consorted with
saloon girls?*

"My shop's right across from the saloon," Miss
Susan reminded her. "Many's the time I'd work late
on a wedding dress or some such, and I'd see Charles
coming down those stairs from the rooms above the
saloon where those girls—"

"I know what they do. And I've heard men can
smoke opium up there…" Her head was reeling with
the idea of Charles going there—and with the idea that
she might have married such a man.

It was nearly noon before Charles Ladley descended
the stairs at Ladley House.

"About time you showed your face," his father said,
from his desk in his study, which faced the landing.
"Been out late celebrating?"

Charles started at the voice, freezing at the bottom of the stairs, and rubbed his eyes. His head felt like someone was hammering horseshoes inside it. "G-good morning, Father. I thought you'd be out at Miller's ranch."

"Your mother said she heard you come in at dawn, and I thought I'd wait and ask you what happened. You look like the dickens, boy. Do I take it you and Delia finally—" he sniggered "—sealed the deal, so to speak? Did you set a date?"

He'd hoped his father would be out of the house and he wouldn't have to tell him yet. "I didn't stay at Delia's. I went to Flora," he said, knowing his father was well-acquainted with the saloon girl.

His father's eyes narrowed. "There's more."

Charles's stomach twisted. "Delia's only putting in a thousand. And she told me she won't marry me."

His father's jaw dropped, his face turning blotchy. "Won't marry you? She adores you! You merely haven't been persuasive enough, boy."

Charles shook his head, remembering the finality of Delia's words. "She told me she doesn't—can't— love me that way."

The mayor's eyes bulged in their sockets. "You can't just *accept* that like a meek little lamb! We need her money!"

Charles's eyes clenched shut in misery at the contempt in his father's voice. "I—I'm sorry, Father...."

"Sorry won't get us control of her fortune!" Charles Ladley Senior's voice was like the crack of a whip.

"I'll get her back, Father, I swear it. I'll find a way...."

* * *

Delia was sitting on the porch when Jude rode up. Dressed in pearl-gray silk with contrasting bands of charcoal-gray at the hem and wrists, her hair curling loosely down her back, she looked so lovely that his throat tightened.

"New dress, Delia? It's very pretty," Jude said, dismounting. *Was she wearing it to go to dinner with Ladley?*

"Thank you. Yes, it's new." She stood, watching him intently as he strode up the walk.

"Were you…going somewhere?" he said, pausing at the top of the steps. "I won't stay if you were… I… Mrs. Heston's probably got dinner ready.…"

Her eyes were luminous in the early evening light. "I saw her in town today, and told her you might be late. Come inside—I have something I want to tell you."

Was he going to have to listen to her tell him she'd accepted a proposal of marriage from Ladley? Was she so oblivious to his feelings that she'd expect him to wish her happy?

Climbing the last step and following her inside seemed like scaling the highest mountain. His heart beat like a trip-hammer.

Closing the door behind them, she took his hand in hers. "I want you to know I told Charles last night I couldn't marry him."

Could he have heard her right? "Why?" was all he managed to say, drowning in the green, fathomless depths of her eyes as she looked into his face.

"Because I love *you,* Jude Tucker. I…I don't know what you'll do about it—maybe it won't change your mind about going back to Nevada, but that's the reason."

"Oh, Delia, I love you, too." Afterward, neither of them were ever sure which of them opened their arms first, but it was some time later when he said, "I was a fool not to have started courting you the day we met. But why would you have trusted *me,* a man you'd just met, who came to tell you your father was dead and you were rich? I'd have sounded like nothing more than a fortune hunter."

Delia looked thoughtful. "I did trust you, though. I don't know why. Maybe it's why I was so forward, inviting you to dinner at the hotel. I wanted to hear more about my father, yes—but I wanted to get to know *you,* too."

"I *wanted* to accept," he admitted, cupping her cheek. "I didn't think it would be good for you…that *I* would be good for you. I'm still not so sure, Delia. The good Lord's been working on me, but I'm still a poor man—"

"That doesn't ma—"

He interrupted her before she could say that his lack of money didn't matter, because she had to know the rest. "And a minister who very nearly committed adultery with another man's wife."

Delia's eyes widened.

He gestured for them to sit down on the couch. "I didn't know Nora was married when I met her," he said, watching Delia's face, hoping he wouldn't see the glorious new love for him fade. "She told me she was a widow, and I began helping her out at her farm, which she was barely keeping going by herself. I would have done anything for her. She kept dangling herself as the prize...." He looked away then, shamed anew. "Then her supposedly dead husband returned from the war."

Delia's eyes never left his.

"She said if I'd kill him, she'd not only give herself to me that very night, but she'd marry me. For a few moments, I was actually tempted," he admitted. "But then it was as if I suddenly woke up. I left that farm that very night."

She'd gone pale, taking it in.

"That's why I told you I can't go back to being a preacher. You can still love me, knowing what I almost did?" he asked, and was shaken to see her nod.

"The important thing was you *didn't* go through with it," she told him. "I'll love you, no matter what you choose to be, but I still think you ought to go back to preaching—right here in Llano Crossing. Oh, you'll have to tell the church board what you told me," she said, holding up a hand when he would have protested. "But God's forgiven you, and I believe He still wants you preaching the Word."

"I—I'll have to think about that, Delia—*pray* about it," he said. "But do you really think a board headed by Charles Ladley Senior is going to accept me?" he asked.

"Especially if you're marrying the woman his son was courting, you mean?" she asked, sobered at the thought, but she stopped as she saw him grin. "What's so funny?"

"Why, Delia Keller, I believe you just proposed to me," he drawled.

Her jaw dropped open, but then she began to smile. "Why, Jude Tucker, I believe you're right. It seems I can't stop being forward around you."

He kissed her again. "And I accept. But we're going

to do this properly. I'm going to court you, Delia Keller, and we're going to pray about it, and about whether I should be a preacher again, and—"

"I wouldn't have it any other way."

Chapter Twenty

Delia awoke at dawn smiling. Her world had changed completely last night, and now she knew what joy really meant. It hadn't consisted of having enough money to buy anything she wanted or being able to move into the house of her dreams soon. It had nothing to do with being worthy of marrying into a socially prominent family like the Ladleys. She had achieved those things, and they had left her empty and uncertain inside, because she had forgotten about depending on God.

It had everything to do with knowing she had the love of a good man, a man who was finding his way back to serving God and who would help her to do the same. Whether Jude became a preacher again, remained a carpenter or whatever he did, the Lord would be the head of their house.

She only had one unpleasant task to do before she felt entirely free to enjoy her happiness. Rising before she heard Miss Susan stirring in the other bedroom, she gathered together the things Charles had given her—earbobs, a crystal vase, a gold brooch and the riding habit Mrs. Ladley had lent her. She had to return these things to him, and she wasn't looking forward to it. Perhaps she could leave them with his mother? But had Charles even told her what had happened?

She regretted that ending her relationship with Charles would probably mean the end of her burgeoning friendship with Jane Ladley. The mayor's wife seemed to be a genuinely nice, motherly lady, and because she loved her son, she might well see Delia now as the woman who had hurt Charles.

"Don't put yourself through that, Delia. I'll walk over to the Ladley house and drop those things off before I open the shop," Miss Susan offered as they walked to town, when Delia explained what was in her poke. "You know he'll try to wheedle his way back into your good graces."

Delia feared exactly that—or that he might have grown angry and say rude things to her, especially if they were alone together at his home. "Thanks, but it would be cowardly of me."

"Well, you won't have to walk to his house, Delia," Miss Susan said, as they neared her shop. "He's coming out of the bank. Want me to stay?"

Charles had spotted her and was walking toward her. He'd probably not appreciate a witness to their conversation. "No, and don't let him see you watching from the window," Delia said. Shrugging, Miss Susan went around to her back entrance.

"Delia! You're looking beautiful this morning. I'm glad to run into you," he said, smiling at her as if nothing had happened. "See, everyone's buzzing about the gold-mine project," he added, nodding toward a knot of men talking excitedly in front of the saloon across the street.

"Good morning, Charles," she said, taken aback by his cheery demeanor. She kept her voice pleasant, even. "I...I have some things to give back to you."

He froze. Some of the color faded from his face, and for a moment she thought he wouldn't take the sack from her. He looked inside. Pain swam in his dark eyes as he lifted them to her.

"Delia, sweetheart, these were gifts. I wanted you to have them. I still do."

"I can't keep them, Charles. It wouldn't be right. And please thank your mother for the loan of her riding habit."

He took her hand before she realized what he was doing.

"Delia, I'm not giving up on us. You loved me—I know you did—and you will again. Please keep these things, and let them remind you of me," he said, trying to hand the sack back.

She took a step back, freeing herself. "I can't, Charles. And please believe that I won't be changing my mind. Again, I'm sorry, Charles, but I—"

"You will change your mind," he told her with a brittle confidence. "And don't forget about the meeting at the church Wednesday night, when everyone is bringing their pledged money. I'll see you there, right?"

Delia blinked. After the conversation they'd just had, he expected her to attend?

"I—I'll write a draft at the bank and leave it there for you," she told him stiffly. "Goodbye, Charles." She was shaken at the way he'd seemed determined to ignore her resolve. Hoping he didn't see her trembling, she walked into the bank. He was gone when she came out.

Having decided to bake a cake for Jude, she went into the general store for baking chocolate. Just as Charles had said, everyone inside was chattering about the Llano Crossing gold mine and what they were going to do with their shares of the profits. She heard boasting about how much some would pledge—or how hard their men would work to mine the gold. Delia was glad it was none of her concern.

"I'll be painting the rooms inside your house for the next few days," Jude told Delia as she sliced the chocolate cake into pieces for him, Miss Susan and herself.

"Can you borrow the wagon and pick me up at Miss Susan's shop? I can help you paint," Delia told him, delighted that the house was so near completion.

"Pick us both up here," Miss Susan said. "I reckon I can close the shop for the day and wield a paintbrush."

"We can bring a picnic lunch, too," Delia said.

Jude grinned. "Sounds like a good deal to me."

"Remember, we're not painting the dining room or the parlor," Delia reminded him. "I have wallpaper on order from the mercantile. Oh, what if it doesn't arrive in time for Thanksgiving dinner?" she said and fretted.

"We're having wallpaper instead of turkey?" he asked, so seriously that both women giggled.

"Jude, a bare wall in the dining room just wouldn't be very festive. Oh, and tell the Hestons they're invited to Thanksgiving dinner," she told Jude.

"Lucy will want to bring something, so I'll tell her to discuss that with you."

"Tell her I'm making the pies," Miss Susan chimed in. "It's so nice to have folks to bake for."

* * *

Later, as Jude and Delia sat together on the porch, realizing it would soon be too chilly to sit outside, Delia asked, "Am I doing the right thing?"

"Sitting out here holding hands with me? Absolutely, I believe you are, Delia honey."

"I love it when you call me that. No, I mean the house. If you're going to be the preacher, maybe I should sell it, and we'll just stay here," she said, nodding toward the house behind her. "I can't believe I ever let *things* become so important to me. All I want now is to be the very best preacher's wife that ever was."

"And you will be," Jude said, smiling at her in approval. "But, honey, God doesn't disapprove of His children using the blessings He sends, including money. I'm thinking that big house could be a blessing, not only to the Tucker family," he said, smiling at that, "but to others in need—travelers, folks in need, orphans—whoever the Lord sends. Not to mention the babies I hope the Lord will bless us with. If we do even half of that, this two-bedroom parsonage would soon seem very small." He grinned as Delia smiled shyly, sensing she was blushing in the dark. His heart swelled with love and thankfulness that God had seen fit to bless him with this woman's love.

"That all sounds wonderful," she agreed. "Will it be all right if Miss Susan continues to live with us for as long as she wants?"

"Of course," he said, surprised she even thought she had to ask. "Delia, you're a good woman."

Then she told him about her encounter with Charles that morning, her brow furrowing as she described it.

"Try not to worry, honey," Jude told her. "Today he

may not believe you mean it, but as the days go on and you don't change your mind, he'll understand—especially when he sees us at church together and so forth."

"But is that wise?" she said. "You're going to speak with the church board about becoming the new preacher, and his father is the chairman—"

Jude laid a finger on her lips. "Delia, I'm not going to pretend I don't love you. The Lord will work all these things out. If He means for me to be the preacher here, I will be. But there's something I have to investigate first." He told her he was going to apply for a job as a miner as soon as the committee started hiring after Thanksgiving.

"Why?"

Then he told her about his suspicion that there was no genuine gold in the cave. "I'm going to find out. Who better than someone who's been a miner? I know the difference between fool's gold and the real thing."

Her eyes widened with alarm. "You think the committee's out to defraud the town? How could they get away with it? They'd be found out sooner or later."

"And by then they could be miles away with the money. I hope I'm wrong," he admitted. "But does it seem logical that a man like Dixon Miller, whom Heston says has never cared a lick about anyone but himself, suddenly wants to share wealth with everyone in Llano Crossing?"

"No, nor any of the others," Delia murmured, her eyes troubled. "Oh, I *wish* I hadn't pledged anything! I wonder if it's too late to get it back?"

"I'd leave it as it is," he advised. "We don't want them to get wind of the fact that anyone's skeptical. If this *is* fraud and we can catch them at it, I'm hoping everyone can get their money back."

"Oh, Jude, be careful," she said, knowing she couldn't dissuade him from his investigation. "These men could be dangerous—especially Miller and his cowboys."

"I will be," he promised her. "Remember Who we've got on our side."

Chapter Twenty-One

October blended seamlessly into November. Sumac bushes turned red as Moses' Biblical burning bush as Delia's house neared completion. Jude had secured the loan of the Hestons' carriage horse, which was also saddle-broken, and Delia spent almost each day there with Jude, painting, wallpapering and supervising the placing of the new furniture as it arrived. She left in time to accompany Miss Susan home from work and fix supper for the three of them—or sometimes they would go to the Hestons', for the old couple seemed to have appointed themselves as honorary grandparents.

Miss Susan had taken her aside at one point and told Delia that she'd be moving back to the boardinghouse when Delia moved into her new house. "For you'll be getting married soon after that, I don't wonder, and newlyweds need their privacy."

Delia urged her to change her mind. The new house was a big one, she reminded her, and she and Jude wanted it to be a blessing for others, too. They would have room for her for as long as she wanted it.

The older woman's eyes had welled up and she'd

hugged Delia, saying she'd stay until Delia and Jude married, at least, for she didn't want Delia to be lonely in that big house by herself.

Delia heard nothing from Charles. He looked away from her whenever their paths crossed. Jude's reading of the Scripture passage and commenting upon it had become a regular part of Sunday services, and Jude had told her that Charles never looked up when Jude was in the pulpit. Mayor Ladley was frigidly civil to both of them. Much to Delia's amazement, Mrs. Ladley never failed to greet her with a kind smile, but her husband always tried to hurry her past.

Delia would have felt complete relief that Charles had accepted her decision to end their relationship, except that she never saw him with another girl—and there had been times when, alone in town or outside both the parsonage and her new house, she had felt the sensation of being watched.

She never saw anyone, of course, just felt that prickling at the back of her neck....

Delia moved into her new house on the Monday before Thanksgiving and had barely had time to get her kitchen arranged before the day of the big feast.

Thanksgiving dinner was a hearty success. With a little guidance from Lucy Heston and Miss Susan, the turkey was roasted to perfection, and the table groaned under the weight of it and all the traditional side dishes—and all of them groaned with satisfaction afterward. There had been enough food for a battalion, and all that was left of the turkey was bare bones.

Jude pushed himself away from the table after politely declining a second slice of pumpkin pie. "Thanks, but I've let my belt out to its last notch now."

"Yep, I reckon that was the best meal we'll eat this side of Heaven," Mr. Heston chimed in.

"The committee's going to start hiring for the mine tomorrow," Jude reminded them, as they sat in the parlor later.

"Still plannin' to ride out there and apply, are you?" Heston asked.

"Oh, Jude, be careful," Delia said, unconsciously twisting a fold of her skirt of dark purple silk.

Two of Dixon Miller's cowboys lounged indolently on the front porch of the big house, looking harmless enough except for the gun belts they wore. Jude joined the line of applicants that snaked into the house and out onto the winter-brown lawn. Known to most of them now from church, Jude chatted with them while they waited. He learned that most of them had not been able to pledge much, if any, money for the project at the meeting run by the Committee for Civic Improvement, and were hoping to help their families by signing on as miners, but no one except Jude had ever actually done any mining before.

"You're sure t' be hired, then," a wiry graybeard said a little enviously, after hearing Jude had mined silver out in Nevada. "They'll want a man with experience. Mebbe they'll even make you foreman."

But Jude was not made foreman, when it came his turn to be interviewed in Dixon Miller's study. As he stood facing Miller, Amos Dawson, Barton Jeffers and both Ladleys, all seated behind a gleaming pecanwood desk, and another of Miller's henchmen, standing with a gun belt slung low on his hips, he was told his services weren't needed.

"But…but I have experience," Jude protested, allowing himself to look shocked, though he wasn't completely surprised about being rejected. It only strengthened his conviction that something was amiss. "I'm the only one in that line who can say that. Wouldn't you gentlemen like to hire someone who's actually *been* a miner?"

"Mr., ah…Tucker, was it?" Miller made a big show of peering through his spectacles at the application paper Jude had filled out. "Yes, that's it, Tucker. You have to understand, this project was meant to benefit the Llano Crossing residents. You're an outsider."

"But…but you know I've been living here since August," Jude protested, though he already knew it was futile. Charles Ladley was already smirking.

"And did you invest in the project?" Mayor Ladley retorted, reaching for a list on the desk and studying it. "No, your name's not on here."

"I'm a carpenter, not a wealthy man. Most of the men out there aren't on that list, either," Jude argued, jerking a hand in back of him to indicate the line of applicants outside. His sudden motion had the armed man standing behind the seated men straightening and fingering the handle of his pistol in its holster meaningfully. Jude ignored him. "That's why most of us are applying for jobs—we need work."

"But they're longtime citizens," Ladley told him with a sniff. "Whereas *you* drifted into town only recently."

"I've worked for several of the townspeople, including James Heston—a longtime resident—and Mr. Miller's former neighbor," Jude shot back. "Doesn't that count for something?"

"I'm afraid not," Dixon Miller said, with a depre-cating smile.

Jude let his shoulders slump in apparent defeat. "I don't know how I'm going to make it through the winter."

"Perhaps you ought to consider riding on…to greener pastures, shall we say?" Dixon Miller suggested with insincere concern.

Charles Ladley snapped the reins over the carriage horse's rump with unnecessary sharpness as they pulled away from Dixon Miller's grand house. Startled, the horse half reared, then lurched into a trot.

"Take it easy, Son!" his father, next to him, snapped. "I certainly taught you to drive better than that!"

Charles bit back a sharp reply. "Sorry, Father. It's been a long day."

So it had. As the sun sank behind a pair of blue hills in the distance, all the men needed for the gold mine had been hired—the ones to construct the timber shoring, the dynamiters, the excavators, the ones to pan the creek and the river, the ones to guard the creek and the river from outsiders. Panning would start immediately, to take advantage of the milder pre-Christmas weather, but the actual work in the mine had been set to start in February, once the ground had thawed.

"Cat got your tongue?" Charles Ladley Senior said, interrupting his son's thoughts. "You ought to be feeling some satisfaction, giving Jude Tucker his comeuppance. Or are you still riled because Delia Keller showed you the door in favor of a mere jack-of-all-trades? There's plenty of women for you, my boy—you might as well wait for a spicy little *señorita* in Mexico."

Charles glared at his father's bare-faced bluntness. The old man's condescending tone grated on Charles's nerves. "I don't think you realize Tucker could do more than just wreck my chances with Delia Keller," he snapped. "I think we ought to get rid of him."

"What're you saying?" his father demanded uneasily. "You can't mean…"

"What I *mean*, Father, is that Tucker is the only man who's got the knowledge to blow this whole plan up in our faces! Like he said, he's been a miner! And guarding the mine to keep him from snooping may not be enough. If we don't get him out of the way, we won't be sitting pretty on our *estancia* in Mexico—we'll be languishing in a cell in Huntsville Prison."

"But…*murder?* Son, it's too risky. I know you're a good shot—the Yankees certainly had reason to rue your skills—but I'm not sure I trust the committee enough not to open their mouths."

Honestly, the old fool was heading into his dotage! "We don't need to inform them. All I have to do is set up an ambush for Tucker—something I did all the time when I was a sniper in the war, remember. Easy, neat, no loose ends."

His father harrumphed. "I don't want to know anything about it," he said.

Chapter Twenty-Two

November had given way to December, and one afternoon nine days before Christmas, Mrs. Ladley surprised Delia by paying a visit to her new home.

"I hope I'm welcome, Delia. Charles and his father don't know I'm here, but I've missed you and I don't know why we shouldn't continue to be friends, even though I'm not to be your mother-in-law." Her face was sad as she said the last thing, but Delia was warmed by the fact that she'd wanted to come and welcomed her into the parlor, which was now decorated for Christmas. Branches of red possumhaw berries wove themselves among candles on the mahogany mantel, and a sprig of mistletoe Delia had plucked from a mesquite tree hung from the doorway. Jude had dug up a juniper tall enough to touch the high ceiling as their Christmas tree and they had decorated it only the night before.

"Were those ornaments your grandfather's, Delia?" Mrs. Ladley asked as she sipped the cup of tea Delia had poured for her.

Delia shook her head. "A couple of them were my mother's," she said, pointing to a small, carved angel of wood and a cobalt-blue glass ball with only a tiny crack in the back. "When Grandpa was alive, we usually just made paper chains and popcorn string decorations. Most of the ornaments are from the mercantile. Mr. Dean was kind enough to order them for me from Fredericksburg."

"Those German immigrants make the loveliest ornaments. I suppose it's because the Christmas tree came from their country," the mayor's wife said and sighed. "I guess it's up to the women and children to make Christmas what it should be this year—every man in town is so wrapped up in this gold-mining project. It's all they talk about. You can't imagine how much time the committee's spending in meetings these days."

"I hear there's to be improvements for the town with all the money the gold will bring in," Delia said. "A public park with a bandstand, a new town hall, and they'll enlarge the church..."

"I'm thinking they'd better wait until that money starts rolling in, don't you?" Mrs. Ladley said, rolling her eyes. "Men! Well, hopefully when all these things start happening, we can finally get a new preacher. I just can't understand why all our inquiries haven't brought us one," she fretted. "Especially since you're having the parsonage renovated at your own expense. That's so generous of you, dear."

"I'm honored to be able to do it. And I suppose the right man just hasn't offered himself yet," Delia murmured, forbearing to tell her that Jude was going to offer himself for the position one day or that he'd had plenty of time to work on the parsonage since he'd been turned down by the mine hiring committee. She wondered how much of his rejection had been pure spite on the Ladley men's part, and how much because there was no real gold that would be found—the committee realized Jude would know that as soon as he went down into the cave.

"Are you going to the Nativity play Wednesday night?" Mrs. Ladley asked.

Delia nodded. "It'll be fun to be just a member of the audience this time, not directing it as I always did when Grandpa was alive. I'm so grateful Mrs. Purvis took over the rehearsals this year since I was so busy with building the house."

The grandfather clock in the corner of the room began to chime.

"Dear me, look at the time," Mrs. Ladley said, rising. "Four o'clock already! I must be going, dear. Charles will be wanting his supper before you know it."

Delia bid her a warm goodbye, suspecting that neither Mr. Ladley nor his son knew that she had come.

Sitting in the darkened, crowded church with Jude by her side and watching the story of Christmas being played out before them was like seeing it for the very first time herself, Delia thought.

There were cries of delight as a young girl appeared onstage, stumbling over the long hem of her white cotton angel dress, her golden wings and halo wobbling dangerously as she announced, "Fear not, Mary, for thou hast found favor with God…"

Delia and Jude chuckled along with the rest of the audience as one of the sheep, borrowed from a local farmer, bleated and tried to escape from the stage, which set the burro braying, which in turn made the heifer tethered to the leg of the piano begin to bawl.

But everyone howled when three other boys dressed in improvised Magi robes (which looked suspiciously like Mrs. Purvis's old brocade curtains) and turbans made of towels, complete with borrowed jewels stuck in the centers, marched in leading calves to whose backs had been fixed makeshift humps of burlap to make them look like camels.

"Where is the newborn King that we may worship Him?" the oldest boy, whose voice was beginning to crack on the edge of manhood, asked. "For we have seen His star in the east and bring him gold, frankincense and…and…"

"Myrrh!" Mrs. Purvis stage-whispered from the front row.

"And myrrh!" the boy completed his question triumphantly to another boy playing Herod. Herod had been rendered sinister by a scary-looking fake mustache and beard. It was the same Christmas story, ever wonderful, ever new, ever inspiring.

If only there wasn't that shadow on the horizon caused by the possibility that the committee was arranging an enormous swindle to bankrupt most of its trusting citizens. Jude had told her that he was going to find a way to sneak into the cave some night soon to find out for himself just what, if anything, was down there.

What if he was caught by the committee's henchmen? They could kill Jude and no one might ever be the wiser. Delia shuddered at the possibility.

"Are you all right, sweetheart?" Jude asked solicitously, his face turned toward her in the flickering shadows formed by the row of lanterns that made the stage lighting.

"Sure. I...I just felt a draft," she said, not wanting to tell him about her fears and spoil the magic of the age-old story of Jesus' coming.

"Fear not, for I bring you tidings of great joy," an angel, whom Delia recognized as one of the Dean girls, announced.

Fear not. The words resounded in Delia's heart. God would protect Jude, and he *would* succeed. All the Christmases to come would be more peaceful in Llano Crossing because of Jude's brave investigation.

The sun had already begun to sink into the western hills in late afternoon. Jude was thoughtful as he rode Shiloh along the fence line that separated the road from Miller's ranch, eyeing the fencing that now circled a thick grove of cottonwoods and oak trees on Miller land.

A tough-looking pair of grim-faced, rifle-toting *hombres* stood guard at the entrance. Miller was taking no chances, Jude mused, that someone might want to come explore the mine on his own—and maybe pocket away some of the alleged gold. Jude would have given much just to be invisible for the few minutes it would take to shimmy down into the cave with a pickax and a lantern and see for himself what was down there. Of course, his tools would have to be invisible, too.

Originally, the cave entrance was in the grove that had been on the edge of Miller land where it bordered the Hestons' ranch; now it was all Miller's.

The nugget Morrison had displayed at the meeting had been assayed and proven to be genuine gold, but Jude figured it had been planted, along with a few other nuggets and flakes that some of the investors who had been hired as panners had found in the creek.

Shiloh sidled and pawed the ground. Jude felt that same tingling down his spine Delia mentioned she'd been feeling lately. He knew the guards were watching him, but this was closer—

A shot rang out and Jude crumpled in the saddle. Consciousness ebbing, feeling the warm blood dripping over his face, he clung to Shiloh as the horse plunged and whinnied in alarm.

Help me, God! Then he felt a scorching pain in his shoulder a heartbeat before the second report blasted his ears. He grabbed desperately at Shiloh's mane as a wave of dizzying blackness washed over him, and he went boneless as a sawdust doll over his horse's neck.

"Got him!" Ladley leaped from his concealed perch in one of the thick-leafed oak trees. "And about time! I knew he'd show up sooner or later, nosing around, but I was getting tired of sitting up here waiting like a vulture."

"Looks like ya did," Donley Morrison said, from a sturdy nearby branch, peering through a spyglass. "But there goes his horse with him," he said, as the buckskin whirled and took off back toward Llano Crossing. "Shouldn't we follow and make sure he's dead?"

"No need. Did you see all that blood? Tucker's dead, all right—or will be in minutes. He'll probably collapse off his horse before he reaches town, and if the bleeding doesn't kill him, exposure will. This couldn't have happened better—when he's found he'll be off Miller land and no one can prove who shot him. I'm heading for the saloon—can I buy you a drink? Killing's thirsty work."

Chapter Twenty-Three

Church mouse no more, Delia thought as she stared into the mirror. The image that stared back at Delia from the mirror was that of a confident woman whose eyes and face were lit with the radiance of love. Her hair was parted in the middle and clusters of curls were held back from her face with ivory combs.

"You've outdone yourself, Miss Susan," Delia said, gazing down at the dress she wore of dark green bengaline with scarlet satin piping, then back at the older woman who stood at the doorway of her room.

"Thank you." Miss Susan beamed with pride at her work. "You look so Christmassy. Jude's going to say you're pretty as a picture."

"If he ever gets here," Delia said with a sigh, as the grandfather clock chimed the hour downstairs. "I thought he'd be back by now. He said he had something to do, but he didn't say what."

"Christmas is coming," Miss Susan reminded her. "Don't fret, I'm keeping dinner warm on top of the oven. That ham's going to be tasty. You and Jude have something special planned for tonight?"

Delia felt her cheeks flush. "We were going to talk about setting a date."

"Oh, sweetie, I'm so happy for you," Miss Susan said, coming forward and embracing her, then she straightened. "I hear someone coming," she said, and both women went to the window that faced the road.

In the gathering dark they could see not Jude on his horse, but a man in a buckboard wagon pulling to a stop in front of her house and clambering down from the driver's seat.

"It looks like Mr. Heston," Delia murmured. "What on earth…"

As she hurried for the stairs, she heard pounding at her door, and Heston's voice calling through it, "Delia? Anyone home?"

"Yes, I'm coming!" she called back. "What is it, Mr. Heston?" she asked as she threw the door open.

The old man's face was grim in the lamp-lit foyer. "Delia, you need to come with me. Jude's horse showed up a few minutes ago with Jude hanging over his neck, passed out. He…he's been shot."

The words made no sense. "*Shot?* Jude's been shot? Who did it? Why?"

"I don't know, but I have my suspicions. We can talk about it on the way. He's asking for you," Heston told her. "I've already stopped to summon the doctor, so he should be there by now."

"Oh, dear Lord," Delia said, feeling the floor shift beneath her feet. For a moment she thought she might faint, and then she felt Miss Susan holding on to her, bracing her.

"I'm coming, too," the seamstress said. "Let me just grab our wraps…"

"Where is his wound?" Delia demanded, as Miss Susan helped her into her coat and threw on her own.

"He has a graze wound to his head and a bullet went through his shoulder. He's lost a lot of blood from that one, Delia," Heston said, as he assisted her and Miss Susan up onto the buckboard. Miss Susan sat in the wagon bed behind them.

The chill that raced through Delia had nothing to do with the brisk winter wind. Would Jude die before she could reach his side? *Lord, please save him!*

"Where did this happen?"

Heston snapped the reins and the two carriage horses took off. "He told me he was riding along the road that runs past Miller's land, in front of the cave entrance, and all of a sudden shots rang out. He didn't see where they were coming from."

That meant he'd regained consciousness and was able to tell Heston what happened.

"It's a wonder he was able to hold on long enough for that stallion a' his to carry him back to our house," Heston told her, almost shouting to be heard above the drumming of the horses' hooves. "Or he'd be lying out there somewhere, still bleeding—or Miller's men woulda finished him off," Heston told her, keeping his eyes on the road as he snapped the reins to speed up the horses.

They managed to get though town without passing anyone. It seemed like an eternity before the wagon pulled up in front of the Hestons' little house. Delia spent it praying. *Please, God, let him live! Oh, Lord, why would they want him dead?*

"You go on in, Miss Delia—he's in the back bedroom," Mrs. Heston called from the doorway. Delia jumped down and ran inside, barely aware that Miss Susan remained behind with Mrs. Heston in the kitchen.

Jude was lying on his back in the shadowy room, his unshaven face looking drawn and almost as bleached of color as the bandages around his head and the top of his left shoulder. His eyes were closed but flew open as Delia ran into the room and up to the bed.

"You...you came," Jude said, as if it were a miracle.

"Of course I came," she said, spotting Doc Jones sitting on the other side of the bed as she sank onto her knees. "Oh, Jude, you might have been killed," she cried, staring at him, seeing the tiny splotch of dried blood that had come through the layers of bandage on his shoulder.

He shook his head at her last exclamation. "God's not finished with me yet."

Doc Jones stood. "He should recover, if infection doesn't set in," he said. "I'll just step out into the kitchen for a minute while you talk. But not for too long," he cautioned.

"Mr. Heston told me you didn't see who shot you," she said, still staring at his pale face. "Jude, you have to stop this investigating. The committee's apparently so determined to keep their secret they're willing to kill. I think you should leave town—"

"It's too late now," he said. "They know I'm onto them. No, I have to find a way into that mine when it isn't guarded. Get a sample somehow. I can tell in a minute if it's fool's gold or not—pyrite flakes into crystals, for one thing, and there's black streaks running through it, where real gold has yellow streaks. Maybe there's nothing down there at all, unless it's more planted nuggets."

Her mouth dropped open. "Jude, you're *badly wounded,*" she said, wondering if the doctor had given him some laudanum that was making him talk out of his head. "You're in no shape to be exploring caves."

"I'll mend in a few days," he told her. "Well enough to get down there, anyway. I've got to see for myself before we can report this to the state police," he said, referring to the force that had taken the place of the Texas Rangers in the state's Reconstruction government. "Sheriff Jenkins is on the committee, you know, so we can't trust him."

She saw that she wasn't going to change his mind. "Could you get down there at night?"

"If it's guarded during the day, it's probably guarded at night, too," Jude countered. "Particularly now that they've shot me for getting too close."

"We've got to tell everyone you're shot worse than you are, that you'll probably die," Delia said, her mind somehow operating very clearly in spite of the shock that made her tremble like a sapling in a windstorm. "If they think you're going to be up and around in a few days, they might try again," she said flatly. "They might come here—can we trust Doc Jones?"

Jude nodded. "I've already sounded him out on that, and we can. Seems he was doubtful about this gold mine from the start. He's going to let it be known I'm still unconscious, hovering between life and death, and there's nothing he can do but pray," he said in a mock-dramatic tone that failed to bring a smile to Delia's lips.

"What are you planning?" she asked, hardly daring to breathe.

"I'm thinking there'll be guards out there on Christmas Eve just like every other night, but I'm betting they'll be celebrating—" he pantomimed drinking from a bottle "—sure that everyone will be snug in their beds that night," Jude explained. "I'll wait until they're all dead drunk, then sneak past them into the mine."

"I can't let you do that," she said, her chin jutting forward with her determination. "If they catch you, they'll finish killing you! No, I'll call a town meeting and insist the committee hire an official assayer to confirm that there's real gold in the mine. If they refuse, it's as good as an admission of fraud."

He shook his head. "Most of them have gold fever so bad they probably wouldn't believe you. The committee will say that hiring an outsider will bring claim-jumpers. The Llano Crossing folks want so badly to believe they're going to be wealthy just as soon as the mining begins—as wealthy as you."

Chapter Twenty-Four

The congregation's mood was festive, and the church was decorated in fresh greenery on this last Sunday of Advent, Mrs. Heston reported when she returned from church. Delia had stayed at their house along with Mr. Heston, ostensibly to keep vigil by Jude's bedside but also to stand guard in case the committee's henchmen thought to take advantage of the church service and come to finish Jude off. Heston had loaned Delia his pistol; he had his carbine close to his hand.

"Mayor Ladley led the congregation in prayer for your recovery, Jude, and the capture of whatever bandit waylaid you," Lucy Heston told him.

"The blasted hypocrite," growled Heston.

"Part of his prayer is already being answered," Jude said, flexing his injured shoulder experimentally and trying to hide his wince. "It hurts a lot less. I'll be ready to explore that cave Christmas Eve."

"Oh dear," fretted Lucy Heston. "I wish there were some safer way, Jude dear. Maybe we should telegraph the state police instead."

"How do we know the telegraph office isn't controlled by the committee?" Delia pointed out.

"Time enough to telegraph them when we have the Ladleys and their cronies corralled in the jail," Jude said.

"Is Mr. Tucker better?" Mr. Dean asked as Delia paid for her purchases. Mrs. Heston had sent her to the mercantile to buy a few staples she was running short of, and since Delia had been spending most of her time at the Hestons' with Jude, she was happy to run the errand for her. It would allow her to buy a few Christmas presents for the old couple.

"There's no change," Delia said and sighed heavily, keeping her eyes down.

Mr. Dean was studying her sympathetically. Not wanting to meet his gaze, she looked instead down the counter at an elegant black frock coat with matching trousers, a black string tie and complementing gold-figured waistcoat hanging tantalizingly behind the counter. How easily she could imagine Jude, tall and handsome in such an elegant ensemble, preaching from the pulpit, but of course she couldn't tell Mr. Dean that.

"Does he need any laudanum, perhaps?" Mr. Dean suggested, holding up a small dark bottle of the liquid from underneath the counter.

Delia shook her head. "Mrs. Heston still has some for him, thanks," she said, gathering up the rest of the things Dean had wrapped up. "Have a nice Christmas."

"Merry Christmas," Mr. Dean called after her, as she walked out the door.

She hated having to deceive the shopkeeper she'd known forever, but she couldn't admit Jude was nowhere near death's door and risk that he would tell others. Mr. Dean was one of those who'd invested heavily in the gold mine.

It was nearly dark and shops were closing. Delia had only to collect Miss Susan, and they'd walk down to the Hestons' and have dinner with them and Jude. She was going to have to find a way to thank the old couple for taking such good care of Jude and for their hospitality to her, when this was all over.

Passing the bank, Delia stepped off the boardwalk into the narrow road between the bank and the seamstress's shop.

"Hello, Delia," said a voice out of the shadows at the side of the bank. She looked up into the face of Charles Ladley.

"Oh! Charles…" Delia hoped he hadn't seen how he'd startled her, though every nerve had turned to threads of ice at the sight of him. "G-getting close to Christmas, isn't it? Please wish your parents a merry Christmas for me. I have to go—Miss Susan's expecting me," she said, pulling back.

"Is that so?" he asked, his voice on-the-surface pleasant, but something far from pleasant lurked in his dark gaze—something soulless and lethal, like the unblinking stare of a snake.

Delia looked past him to the shop, hoping to see Miss Susan watching for her from her window, but she wasn't there.

"Let me go, Charles," she said levelly, her eyes darting in all directions to see if someone—anyone!—was nearby. But it seemed everyone had gone home for their suppers and the streets were deserted. No one was going in or out of the saloon right now. If anyone was dining at the hotel restaurant, it seemed they weren't sitting near the window.

"Put down your packages and come with me, Delia." He took them from her and dropped them in the dirt.

"Why?"

"I have a little surprise for you. 'Tis the season for surprises, isn't it?" He pulled at her hand, urging her down the narrow road that led toward the river and Jeffers's mill.

Balking, she stared at him, her mind racing. She thought of pretending to faint or, better yet, screaming at the top of her lungs that she was being robbed. Miss Susan would have to hear her and come running—and maybe Mr. Dean, too. Charles wouldn't dare stay and have them find him there.

Pushing her against the building with one hand, he let her see the pistol he had been concealing under his coat. "Come on, Delia," he said. "Don't make me use this."

How had she ever found him handsome? Or kind?

"You are as faithless as you are beautiful, Delia," he went on in a strange singsong. "Do you think I don't know you aren't plotting with Jude Tucker to bring down all we've planned? Is he your lover?" he asked casually, but his eyes bored into hers, glittering.

"No," she said, answering his last question first. "Let me go, and we'll say no more about it, Charles," she said, trying to sound as emotionless as he did. "We won't expose your crooked plot. We'll leave town quietly, this very night," she said, desperately searching his face for some sign of agreement and finding none.

She tried again. "Let me go and we'll go to the bank,

and I'll sign over every cent to you. You'll never hear from us again."

"'Us' meaning you and your *carpenter*." Charles sneered. "You must think me quite a fool to imagine I'd let you run off to Austin and bring the state police down on our heads, Delia, but I'm no fool. You'll be leaving town, all right, but not with Tucker. You'll be departing with me, right now. I took the liberty of going to your house and packing a few things—easy since you've hardly been there of late—and placing them in the landau. We'll head for the border, along with my entourage," he drawled, now nodding toward the two men who stood at both ends of the alleyway, their pistols drawn and cocked. One of them, Delia saw, was Donley Morrison, who smirked at her from the shadows.

"We'll be married right across the border in Matamoros," he told her. "We'll tell everyone we've been reunited, and our love couldn't wait any longer."

"You can't force me to marry you," she said, horror-struck.

"Oh, I think I can," he said. "You think some Mexican *padre* who doesn't speak English will listen to your pleas? My parents will be there, too—we'll have our own little Ladley palace down in Mexico, with the aid of your money and all that's been fleeced from the gullible folk of Llano Crossing."

"Your mother won't agree to this," she hissed. "She's good and kind, everything you're not. How she could ever have given birth to a son like you is a mystery to me."

"She didn't," Charles told her. "I'm the product of my father's liaison with a saloon girl. But Mother's never had to fend for herself, and she'll agree to anything to keep Father and me happy, even moving to Mexico. Once Father brings the money from the 'gold mine'—and the sale of your house—we'll all be one big happy family, far from the reach of the pigeons we've plucked."

Delia could only stare into the face of the man she had once tried to convince herself she loved. That time seemed years ago. Now there was something not quite sane about the way he talked.

Charles lowered the gun and pressed it insistently into her ribs. "Now march down the road here to the carriage like nothing's amiss, or I swear I'll shoot you right here like the faithless woman you are."

There was nothing she could do but comply. She walked to the landau, her legs like jelly. Absently, she noticed that Zephyr and Charles's bay had been tied to the back of the carriage.

He saw her looking at her mare.

"Yes, I'm not leaving a valuable beast like your thoroughbred behind for these yahoos. But abandon any hopes of running away on her, sweetheart. I wouldn't hesitate to put a shot right between her ears and bring her down. And I can do it—I was a sniper in the war. I killed hundreds of Yankees."

While the cowboy-guards mounted their horses, Charles got in beside Delia, keeping his Colt leveled at her but out of sight.

Busy with Christmas preparations, no faces appeared in windows to mark her passing. Llano Crossing might as well have been a ghost town. They would take the road leading south out of town—not the east road that led past the Hestons' house. Jude would not even know she had been taken.

She was numb with terror and hopelessness. If she resisted, he'd kill her. If she complied and allowed him to force her into marriage, her life would be misery beyond imagining.

And call upon Me in the day of trouble: I will deliver thee, and thou shalt glorify Me.

All she could see were the faces of her captors. But she heard the voice in her heart, an echo of all those times her grandpa had her read aloud in the Psalms: "I will call upon God; and the Lord shall save me."

You told me to call if I needed Your help, Lord. You see the danger I'm in. Please do as You promised, and Jude and I will spend our lives glorifying You.

Jude was restless as a red ant under a magnifying glass. He and Heston had talked endlessly about the plan.

"I'm goin' out to the mine site with you Christmas Eve," Heston told him. "It's too dangerous, you goin' alone."

"It's too dangerous for you to go with me," Jude retorted. "No hard feelings, Jim, but do you really think you could crawl under the barbed wire with me?"

"No, I know I can't," Heston shot back. "But what if those guards *ain't* drunker'n boiled owls? You're assumin', son, but what if you're wrong?"

Since it was the same objection Delia had made, it silenced Jude for a minute.

"You wouldn't shoot 'em to get your look in the mine, would ya?"

"No," Jude admitted. He'd give his own life, if need be, to save the woman he loved, but no matter how bad these men were, it wouldn't be right for him to get his evidence that way. "What did you have in mind?" he asked Heston.

"If they ain't three sheets to the wind, I'll stage a diversion. I'll make some noise and draw 'em off, and while they're chasin' after me, you can shimmy down and get your ore samples."

Jude sighed. He'd really hoped Heston had a scheme better than the one *he'd* racked his brain to come up with. "Sorry, but there's no way I'm going to let you do that. Mrs. Heston won't thank me if I get you killed."

Heston's shoulders sagged. "That's what I really hate about getting old," he said. "No one thinks you can do anything."

Jude laid a comforting hand on his boss's shoulder. "You can do a lot of things," he assured him. "And I'm counting on you, if something happens to me, to ride to the next town and telegraph the state police."

"Of course," Heston said. "Hope it doesn't come to that."

"It's up to the Lord to make this succeed," Jude reminded him. "I don't like waiting till Christmas Eve, either. But if my plan doesn't work, or the Lord doesn't want us to wait that long, He's going to have to show us another way."

Together, they bowed their heads.

They had been praying for only a few minutes when Jude was seized by a restlessness he could not explain. Lifting his head, he interrupted Heston in midsentence. "Jim, I've got to go into town and check on Delia. Something's wrong. I can feel it." He pushed the sling down off his shoulder and grabbed for his shirt. He might not be able to use the arm very well, but at least it was his left one. Shiloh was well-trained enough to be guided by his master's knees if Jude had to use his hands. "Lend me a pistol."

"Gimme a minute to load my old Colts. You're not goin' alone, and that's that."

Chapter Twenty-Five

M iss Susan was locking her shop when Jude's stallion, followed closely by Heston's sorrel gelding, slid to a stop in front of her.

"Did you see Delia?" Jude demanded without ceremony.

The middle-aged seamstress goggled up at him, clearly astonished to see him out of the house and on his horse. "An hour ago she poked her head in to say that she was going to buy some things for Mrs. Heston at the mercantile, and she'd stop by to get me afterward. We were coming down to see you. But she never showed up, and the mercantile's closed. I thought maybe she forgot to pick me up, and I was going to walk down to the Hestons' and see—"

"Do you think she might've gone to her house instead?"

The seamstress's brow furrowed in thought. "I can't think why—she'd said we were invited to dinner, right, Mr. Heston?" All at once she peered into the darkness and pointed. "Oh, look," she said, pointing to some small wrapped bundles lying by the side wall of the bank, and before Jude could dismount, she went over and opened them.

"Flour, eggs, sugar...a shaving mug...a crystal dish... She said Mrs. Heston was out of some essentials, and she wanted to buy them some little Christmas presents...."

"Then those things might be hers," Jude said.

"But why would she leave 'em there?" Heston asked.

Both men turned in their saddles to look down the mill road and up the street that led out of town. There was no one outside, and every business but the saloon was dark.

"Where could she be?" Miss Susan demanded. "I saw Charles Ladley walk by sometime before she stopped in here, and he had Donley with him, that scoundrel, and some other cowboy—" The older woman stopped, her eyes widening in horror, just as Jude reached the same conclusion. "Oh, Jude, you don't think he...he..."

The two men exchanged looks.

"I think we'll ride on over to the Ladleys' house and see if they're there," Jude told her. "Can you walk on down and stay with Mrs. Heston?"

Miss Susan nodded, and both men reined their horses around and kicked them into a lope in the opposite direction. Jude was surer than ever that Delia was in danger. But if Charles hadn't brought Delia there, would his parents know where they were—and if they did, would they tell them the truth? Maybe they'd try to steer them wrong deliberately.

No groom came outside to inquire if he could take their horses when they pulled up in the Ladley courtyard. The house was unlocked; no one answered their halloos when they went inside. Then Jude heard a faint thumping coming from the attic. Following the noise, they ascended the stairs and found Mrs. Ladley and Maisie, the cook, trussed up like Christmas geese, gags in their mouths. The two women had been rocking the chairs that they had been bound to against the wall.

Mrs. Ladley's eyes went wide with fear when Jude burst into the attic room. They went wider still when he ran up to her. She whimpered, clenching her eyes shut, clearly almost hysterical with fright, shrinking away from him but unable to scream because of the gag in her mouth as he bent over her.

"I mean you no harm, Mrs. Ladley," he assured her, working at the tight knots to untie her gag. "I'm Jude Tucker, and I only want to know if you've seen Delia. Did your son bring her here? I have reason to believe she's in trouble. Why are you tied up?" he asked, when he was able to pull the knot loose at last.

"Please… I'm dry… Water…" she croaked. Jude ran back downstairs and fetched a pitcher of water and two glasses, while Heston bent to free her and the cook from their bonds.

"Thank God someone finally came," she said, after drinking a glass of water straight down without pausing, while Jude poured another for the cook. "Maisie and I were tied up because I dared to argue when Charles came in here and told me he was going to elope with Delia. He was wild-eyed—crazy-looking. I raised that boy, and I know when he's lying. When I wouldn't shut up, he *pulled a gun on me and Maisie* and herded us up here and tied us up!"

"Where's your husband, Mrs. Ladley?" Heston asked.

She shrugged. "I don't know. He hasn't been here

all day. I know my husband and his son think I'm a witless fool," she went on, "and merely a decoration in this house," she added, chafing her abraded wrists, "but I'm not. I've suspected for a long time that there was something crooked about that so-called gold mine."

"Miz Ladley's right. Dat boy looked crazy as a horned toad with a sunstroke," the cook chimed in.

"Mrs. Ladley, where do you think your son took Delia?" Jude asked her, letting her see his urgency. "Delia wouldn't go with him willingly for any reason, let alone marry him. She was expected at the Hestons' house. I'm afraid Charles may have taken her against her will."

"I don't know," she said, staring up at him, "and that's the honest truth. But my fool of a husband's been careless enough to keep records of the committee's meetings, and I know what they're plotting. There's no gold, Mr. Tucker—unless you count what they planted there and fool's gold enough to keep the townspeople thinking they've found the real thing for a while longer. My husband and his cursed committee are planning to take the money they've stolen from the honest citizens of this town and run off to Mexico and live like kings. But I think my husband and his son have stolen a march on the rest of the committee and taken the money— yes, and maybe Delia—and left his cronies to face the music. And they thought I'd go with them!"

Jude felt no sense of victory at having his suspicions confirmed, only a desperate need to cut through the mayor's wife's tale to get to a clue about Delia.

"So you think Charles and his father have taken Delia with them to Mexico?"

Mrs. Ladley, however, was not to be hurried. Now

that she finally had an audience, she seemed determined to tell her story her way. "Charles and his father have been more and more fearful of discovery as the date of the mine opening drew closer. Yes, I don't mind admitting I listened at keyholes," she said with a bitter laugh. "They realized it was only a matter of time before someone noticed they'd been swindled, and they were determined that Charles would wed Delia first, so they'd have her money, at least, if everything else about the plot failed. This is a fine old house, yes, but I don't mind admitting to you that we haven't had a nickel to spare since the war. We've just been keeping up appearances."

"Mrs. Ladley—" Jude said, trying to interrupt her.

"Charles rather fancied Delia Keller all along," she went on, oblivious, "but of course she was poor as the proverbial church mouse. Charles and his father had decided that in order to resume our proper place in society again, Charles had to marry a rich woman. But when Delia inherited all that money, Charles decided she was good enough for him now, the poor girl! I know I should have warned her," she said sadly, "but I'd hoped she might persuade Charles to become a better man...."

A tear made its way down her wrinkled cheek.

"Mrs. Ladley, I'm sorry that all this happened to you," Jude said, as patiently and kindly as he could despite the exigency that gripped him. He felt pity for this woman, who had apparently endured years of emotional abuse. "But is there anything you can tell me that will help me find Delia? Is your husband with them? Every minute may count, ma'am."

Mrs. Ladley could only shake her head. "I don't know where my husband's gone, Mr. Tucker. But I suspect that his son—" Jude noticed she'd referred to him as "his son," not "our son" "—is going to head for the border and force Delia to marry him in Mexico and set up a home down there where the officials can be bribed to ignore their presence."

Jude turned to Heston. "What lies between here and the border?" he asked. When he'd traveled from Nevada to Llano Crossing, he'd come from the northwest, not the south.

The old man thought for a moment. "Fredericksburg, but other than that, nothin' much between here and San Antone but more little towns like Llano Crossing. After San Antone, though, there's just one main road and not much but cactus and mesquite till the Rio Grande. But if they decided to stop at San Antone…" He shrugged. "There's lots a' places to hole up there, and we'd go right past, thinking they'd gone on south past the city."

"So I've got to catch them before they reach San Antonio, if at all possible."

Heston nodded. He understood without asking that Jude would have to go alone. At his age, he wasn't up to such an arduous fast ride, and Jude couldn't afford to be held back by him.

"Go with God, son. While you're gone, we'll call the townspeople together and tell 'em what's been going on. After I tell them Ladley's kidnapped Delia, they'll believe the whole gold-mine scheme's a fraud, I promise you. We'll round up any of those scalawags from the committee that are still left and stick 'em in the jail."

"I'll be happy to testify against my husband when he's caught," Mrs. Ladley said with quiet dignity. "God keep you safe, Jude Tucker."

"And we'll find some young fella to ride for the law

in Mason, since our own sheriff will be in the jail with the rest," Heston added.

Jude was impressed by their determination, but even so, he felt a jab of despair. Ladley had several hours' head start on him, and darkness had fallen as they reached the Ladleys' house. There wouldn't be enough of a moon out tonight to light his way. Shiloh wouldn't be able to gallop all night, and what if he put a leg into a hole in the road that he couldn't see?

Lord, if You want Delia and I to be together, we're going to need Your help now. You gave the three Wise Men a star to follow so long ago—please, help me, too. Give my horse swift and sure legs. Help Delia not to be scared. I'm not worthy to ask You for anything, but You've assured us that You listen to Your children's cries for help.

Chapter Twenty-Six

While Donley put up the folded bow top on both ends of the landau, Charles wrapped her up warmly with a buffalo robe, every inch the loving beau, then settled himself opposite her with his gun hidden beneath the folds of his own buffalo robe.

Delia said nothing at first, as the landau bowled along over the hilly roads south of town. What was there to say? Begging would do no good. Charles had no heart to be reached. She couldn't bear to look at him. Instead, she kept her eyes on the endless parade of mesquite, cedar, cactus and rolling, rock-studded hills. The sun was fast disappearing behind a mesa on her right side; soon it would be completely dark.

Be strong, and of a good courage.

After another mile or two, she said, "We can't drive all night, you know. The horses won't last. And it looks mighty cloudy up there." She pointed at the sky. "I think it's going to rain."

"Father's meeting us with a brougham—and a fresh team," he told her, laughing at her dismay. "We'll be at the meeting point soon."

A brougham? It was going to be more than a little crowded with the two of them, the mayor and the luggage, too. Perhaps Charles was planning to ride his horse some of the time. But if she was right about the weather, at least she would be more protected from the elements than in his landau.

About half an hour later, they pulled up in front of a black hulking shape in a grove of oak trees. As they drew nearer, the shape revealed itself as the promised brougham hitched to two fresh horses. Charles Ladley Senior got out of it, holding up a hand in greeting.

"You made good time," Mr. Ladley praised his son. "And how's your lovely bride? Good evening, Delia," he greeted her with such effusive cordiality that Delia wanted to spit at him. "Such a romantically thrilling elopement, eh?"

Delia's smoldering anger vented itself in sarcasm. "Not too many eloping grooms have to bring their fathers along for reinforcement. And I see you couldn't talk your wife into joining us on this little romantic getaway, Mr. Ladley."

She wasn't quick enough to avoid Charles's slap, or to control her own instinctive reaction. Fingers curled into claws, she launched herself at him.

Anticipating her fury, he caught her wrists before she could strike him and held her as she thrashed wildly against him while the hired guns swiftly and expertly bound her wrists and ankles then hauled her to the brougham.

Quick tears welled up in her eyes, but she averted her face, not about to let any of them see her cry.

"Mind your tongue, you little shrew," the mayor said,

"or I won't let my son sully the Ladley name by giving it to you."

Chilled to the bone by the elder Ladley's threat, she nevertheless couldn't help but retort, "You've sullied your own name, Mr. Ladley."

For a moment, she thought the mayor was going to strike her, then he turned to his son and snarled, "Let's get going."

Delia sat hunched in despair as the carriage rumbled on through the night. How much did Mrs. Ladley know of the plot, if anything? She hadn't been brought along, but when her husband and son didn't come home, would she raise the hue and cry? Or was she so beaten down by years with her husband that she would wait tamely for her chance to join them in Mexico?

How soon would the town realize they'd been duped and demand to see what was in the mine?

Had Jude realized yet she'd been kidnapped? He'd be out searching for her, regardless of his recent wounds, but he wouldn't know where to look unless Mrs. Ladley had guessed her husband and son's intent to escape to Mexico and told what she knew. How soon would that be? She had no way of knowing.

"Jude Tucker will catch up," she said, as though she believed he was minutes away. "He won't let you get away with this."

"Your lovesick carpenter won't have any idea what's happened to you," Charles said. "And even if he ever figures it out, he'd be too far behind to catch up."

"Yes, he will," she insisted.

"Even if he did, he'd be rather outnumbered, don't you think? Ace and Donley are more than a match for one miner-carpenter," Charles retorted.

Just then Delia heard the first plops of rain fall on the carriage roof, and even inside the carriage she could hear the wind pick up.

"We'd better stop in Fredericksburg and spend the night at the hotel," the mayor told his son, as the plops became more steady.

"I'm not stopping for a little rain," his son snapped. "Fredericksburg's too close to home, if they figure out where we're going!"

"They won't," his father said. "Everyone's so wrapped up with Christmas coming and gold fever, they won't notice if we're missing," he said with a chuckle. "My dear wife's going to be mad as a wet hen when Manuel finally finds her and Maisie all tied up, but she might be so embarrassed she's been left behind that she won't say anything till they come looking for us."

The rain became a drumming, and still the carriage rolled on through the night.

The rain had been falling in spattering, tentative drops that slid down the oilskin duster Jude had dug out of his saddlebag, but a few yards ahead of them, it was falling in undulating sheets of water. In a moment, Shiloh would be running in the thick of the downpour.

Lord, I thought You were going to help me, he thought, despondent as thunder rumbled somewhere behind them. *A downpour will only slow me down.* Shiloh had been making good time, eating up the miles with his far-reaching stride, but Jude knew he'd have to rest his valiant stallion soon. And soon would come sooner in this cloudburst.

If the rain slows you down, Jude, don't you think the rain is going to delay Ladley more? the Voice within him said. Jude had seen Ladley's landau was not in the stable, and Mrs. Ladley said their brougham was missing as well, so he could guess they were in one or the other, rather than on horseback. No carriage could travel as fast as a horse and rider. "Lord," he said aloud, "Shiloh's just about exhausted."

He can go a little farther. Ride on till you find shelter.

Minutes later, horse and rider came to a bend in the road caused by a limestone crag jutting out. Just then lightning flashed and Jude spotted a rocky overhang high and big enough for his horse to stand under. It wasn't much, but it would keep most of the rain off of them while they rested.

"Son, we've got to stop! We can't keep going through this storm all night!" Mr. Ladley said, right after a jagged bolt of lightning struck the ground in the distance and caused the tired team to shy.

His son scowled but gave in. "Find someplace to stop, Ace!" he called to the cowboy up on the driver's seat.

"There ain't no place, Mr. Ladley!" Ace called back in a disgusted voice. "We ain't yet to Fredericksburg, and we're in the middle a' nowhere!"

"Then we'll just have to stop on the road till the worst blows over," the mayor shouted over the drumming of the rain. "We don't dare stop under a tree, with all this lightning!"

"Ain't nothin' around but scrubby little mesquite, anyway!" Ace called back.

The carriage rattled to a stop at the bottom of a hill, the horses blowing and miserable, as wet as if they'd been swimming underwater. Behind the carriage, Charles's bay and Zephyr were in an equally wretched state.

"What about *us?*" Donley demanded, peering into the brougham's window from the back of his horse. He'd been riding behind them, leading Ace's horse. Just like Ace on the driver's seat, he was drenched to the bone.

"Well, there's hardly room in *here,*" Charles said, curling his lip. "Get under the carriage or something!"

Delia saw the cowboy gaze up at his cohort in the driver's seat. A moment later, Ace jumped down from his high perch, but rather than taking Charles's suggestion, he took the reins of his horse from Donley and mounted.

"Hey!" Charles cried as the men reined their horses away from the carriage. "Where are you going?" He pulled out the pistol he'd been clutching all this time. "Stop, or I'll shoot!"

Donley paused long enough to shout over his shoulder, "Ladley, you're *loco!*" Donley and Ace galloped into the inky cascade of rain and disappeared.

"Don't fire, you fool!" his father cried. "The horses will spook and stampede! You can't hope to hit either man anyway!"

Father and son glared at one another, dumbstruck. Delia turned her face away from them, afraid she would laugh and they would turn on her.

"We don't need them, blast their hides," Charles fumed. "We can make it just fine without them." He pulled out his pocket watch and peered at it. "I can't even see what time it is!"

"Got to be after midnight," his father said. "Let's try to sleep until the rain lets up."

Sleep? Delia's muscles were cramped from having her hands and legs tied and not being able to shift and stretch, but she knew it was futile to ask to be untied. Settling herself against the upholstery, she closed her eyes and waited.

Please, Lord, send Jude.

Then, amazingly, she slept.

Chapter Twenty-Seven

Delia woke in the gray light of dawn to the sound of men cursing. The carriage lurched forward, then backward, but didn't move.

Stretching as much as her bonds would allow, Delia blinked and opened her eyes. She was alone in the carriage. Above her, in the driver's seat, she could hear Charles's father swearing at the horses and cracking the whip above them; behind the brougham, Charles groaned and lunged against it.

No one had to tell Delia they were stuck in the mud. Ace had parked the carriage at the bottom of a hill, and the water had soaked into the depression, creating a mire that now held them fast.

"I can't budge it!" Charles grunted, coming past the window to glare accusingly at his father.

"Whip them up—they've got to pull us out of here!" Charles cried, desperation edging his voice. "Maybe if I get Delia out it would be easier for them to pull us free?"

"I've been whipping them! They've been trying, but the beasts just can't do it!" his father snapped back.

"And I don't think moving Delia would make a difference. We're going to have to leave the carriage and go on!"

Charles stared up at his father and then in at Delia. "Come on," he said, opening the carriage and pulling her out, heedless of the way her numb, bound legs made her sag against him and nearly fall. "You're going to have to ride the rest of the way."

Righting herself, Delia faced him and felt her mouth turn up in an impudent grin. She didn't care if he slapped her again—it was worth it to see the frustrated rage on his face.

Instead, however, he took hold of her chin and bent over so that they were practically nose to nose. "Delia Keller, when we get to Mexico, I'll make you pay for every insolent word," he vowed, eyes bulging and red-rimmed. "You will rue the day you were born."

She wasn't about to let him cow her. "Maybe, but first we have to get there, don't we? If you expect me to ride, you're going to have to untie me."

He couldn't argue that. After he'd used a pocket-knife on the rope binding her legs, though, Delia held out her hands, but he only shook his head and pointed at his bay.

"I'm riding your thoroughbred, Delia, so abandon any hope of racing away from me."

"And what about *your father?*" the mayor demanded in an indignant voice.

"Sorry, Father, but you're going to have to ride one of the carriage horses," Charles told him. "Here, take my knife, and cut the harness to make yourself reins."

"You're out of your mind!" Charles Ladley Senior

roared. "The thoroughbred can carry double, and I'll ride your bay."

"The mare can't carry two. She's too skittish. Especially with me loaded down with money," his son argued, reaching into a heavy canvas bag and coming out with both hands clutching fistfuls of gold coins, stuffing them into his pockets until they bulged and sagged. He tied the bag, which still sagged with weight, onto Zephyr's saddle. "That's only a part of your inheritance that Dawson was good enough to draw out for me," he assured Delia. "He'll have the rest transferred, along with the profit from selling your house. We've got to get going. By now we're probably being pursued."

"So leave Delia here, if you're suddenly yellow," his father shouted. "They won't chase us if they can rescue her."

"Sorry, Father, but I've come too far to give Delia— and especially her fortune—up now," Charles told him, cool as the ice that rimmed the nearby puddles of water. "It's your choice—you can either follow on one of the team or you can stay here and wait for Tucker to catch up."

Delia watched, incredulous, as Ladley glared at Ladley. At last, the older man's body slumped. "I should have left you in the saloon with your crazy mother," he growled, glaring at Charles. "You're as mad as she was. Take the girl and go. I won't stay here, but I won't be a part of your insanity, either."

Charles boosted Delia up onto his bay. Beneath her stocking-clad legs, the leather of the saddle was wet and cold.

Taking the bay's reins, he mounted Zephyr. As they rode away, Delia saw that the mayor had cut his mount out of the traces and was struggling to pull himself onto the carriage horse's bare back.

Charles and Delia trotted for perhaps an hour in the bone-chilling damp, the only sound the occasional twittering of birds and the sucking noise as hooves landed in mud and were pulled out again. Try as she might, Delia couldn't hear the sound of any horses behind her.

So Jude wasn't coming or at least he was too far behind them to help her. But they'd have to stop and buy food, and surely she could manage to run away or cry out to someone along the way who would help her. It was still a long, long way to Mexico.

"We're going to avoid the towns," Charles muttered then, almost as if he could read her mind. His eyes gleamed with a light that was no longer reasonable. "When we're hungry, I'll tie you up and go buy food. Between here and the Rio Grande it's mostly poor greasers, anyway, and they'll be happy to earn a few coins."

As if her money mattered now. "What *about* the rest of your committee?" she asked him. "You don't seem very concerned about them. Aren't you worried Dawson won't send the rest of the money to Mexico? And they'll turn state's evidence on you? Or come after you for running out on them with the money?"

He shrugged. "They'll slip away, if they have any sense, my dear Mrs. Ladley."

I'm not your wife yet, and I never will be, she wanted to remind him, but she didn't have the energy. She needed all the strength that remained to keep her knees gripping the bay's sides.

"Ought to be coming to the Guadalupe pretty soon," Charles said conversationally, after they skirted Fredericksburg. They might have been two friends out for a canter in the spring sunshine. "Hopefully there's a bridge, or we'll have to swim for it."

Sure enough, around the next bend, the green water of the Guadalupe River appeared before them. There had been a bridge, all right, but all that remained of it lay in collapsed wreckage on either side. The rain-swollen, rushing river had apparently flooded beyond its banks during the night and taken the bridge with it.

Charles shrugged again, saying with maniacal cheerfulness, "Ah well, it's not as if we could get any wetter by swimming, eh, my love?"

Delia's jaw dropped. Even a madman couldn't imagine they would be able to swim across this river, could he? As she watched, the splintered remains of a ferry platform bobbed past them in the raging torrent.

"Charles, the horses can't swim that," she pointed out, keeping her voice logical and calm. "If we wait awhile and hide out back in the town, the river will go down. A day—maybe less—you'll see."

"But we can't wait, Delia," he responded, just as reasonably. "He's coming."

She paused, listening, but she could hear nothing but the rushing water. Was paranoia consuming Charles?

And then she heard it—distantly, muffled at first, but then she was sure. The sound of a horse's hooves was coming up fast behind them.

"Come on!" he shrieked, as both of them spotted the silver buckskin, with Jude on his back, at the same moment. "We've got to go right now!"

"No!" she screamed, desperately trying to wrench the reins away. "There's no way we'd survive! Charles, I don't want to drown!"

"We can't let him catch us!" he shouted back frantically, trying to kick the mare into plunging into the swift current. He seemed to have forgotten that Delia didn't have the same goal he did—she desperately *wanted* to be "caught."

The bay she rode dug in his heels, pulling away from the other horse. Charles had too much to do to stay on Zephyr to keep hold of the bay's reins, and at last the bay jerked free.

Zephyr continued to resist Charles's commands, bucking and rearing as her crazed rider desperately raked her sides with his spurs. She was struggling to keep her hooves planted on the muddy bank, but it had been weakened by the raging river, and clods of clay kept breaking away into the water.

Just then a report of a gun shook the air, and Delia whipped her head around to see Jude firing, not at Charles but straight up into the air.

The report set the already terrified thoroughbred rearing and plunging, but while she managed to keep from falling into the river, Charles did not. Delia screamed as Charles was catapulted headfirst into the swirling greenish-yellow water.

Charles surfaced almost immediately, yelling and grabbing at branches but weighted down by the coins in his pockets—he couldn't hold on. She had to help him! Dismounting with clumsy haste because her hands were still tied, she tried to grab on to one of the splintered timbers of the bridge, but it was stuck in something beneath the surface of the water and she couldn't pull it loose to extend it to him. She could only watch in horror as he was swept on past.

Jude was still too far away. By the time his stallion slid to a stop beside the shivering mare, Charles Ladley had gone under again. She thought she saw his arm raised, yards down the river, but it may have only been a branch.

And then Jude was pulling her against him, shielding her from what she had just seen, holding her while she wept as if he would never let her go again.

Zephyr was too spent to ride, so Delia rode Charles's bay back to Fredericksburg while Jude, back on Shiloh, led the mare at a walk. Once they reached the town, they went straight to the sheriff's office and told him what had happened, including the fact that Mayor Charles Ladley was still on the loose, probably riding a carriage horse bareback.

The sheriff listened carefully, promising to ride out with his deputies to look for him.

"There's a hotel in town, if you want to rest the horses for the night," the sheriff went on. "Mister, you look plumb played out, if you don't mind my sayin' it, and it *is* Christmas Eve."

Delia blinked. With all that had happened, she had forgotten Christmas was so close.

"Played out" didn't begin to cover it, as far as Jude was concerned. He hadn't slept while waiting out the storm last night, and his wounded shoulder throbbed like a fiery toothache. But as he gazed at Delia, all he wanted was to be at home on Christmas Day with her.

"Reckon we'll push on," he told the sheriff. "We need to notify Charles Ladley's mother about his death. Would it be possible to rent a light carriage at the livery and leave our horses there for a few days?"

"Good idea. One of you can drive while the other sleeps. And if I could make another suggestion, you might take a few minutes to stop over at the mercantile and buy something dry to wear, ma'am. You both look like drowned cats, and it's right nippy out there today after that rain."

Jude smiled, thinking that even with her curls plastered against her face and neck and her dress spattered with mud, Delia still looked beautiful to him.

"You need to borrow some money for the clothes and carriage?" the sheriff asked. "I got some in the drawer here for emergencies."

Jude shook his head and thanked him, explaining that while Charles Ladley's pockets had been weighted down with gold coins, there was still a goodly sum in the bag that had been tied to the thoroughbred's saddle.

"Poor greedy fellow," the sheriff said, shaking his head.

An hour later, having eaten and wearing newly purchased and blessedly dry clothing, Delia and Jude had just reached the edge of town in their rented carriage when they spotted a pair of deputies riding toward them, one of them leading a horse with the remains of a harness still on him, the other leading another horse with an old man in torn, soggy clothing slouching on his back.

Delia gasped, recognizing Mayor Ladley. He looked up at the faint sound, but his eyes were empty and seemed not to recognize her.

At least Charles had taught her to drive a carriage. Now she was thankful that he had, so Jude could doze at her side while she drove into the afternoon.

Jude took over as the early twilight of December darkened the road ahead of them. With the storm having blown eastward, the sky was soon blanketed with stars.

Chapter Twenty-Eight

Llano Crossing seemed as deserted early Christmas morning as it had been when Delia had left. Delia and Jude longed to go to the Hestons' house first to let them know they were safe, but it seemed wrong to pass by Ladley House on the road from the south without going in to tell Mrs. Ladley about her son's death.

When they pulled into the courtyard between the mansion and the stable, however, it was not Mrs. Ladley but Jim Heston who came out to greet them.

"I'm so thankful you're safe," he cried. "Lucy, Miss Susan and I thought it best to wait with her so she wouldn't have to be alone, it bein' Christmas and all." He hesitated, peering at their faces. "I see by your sober faces that you've got some bad news to tell her."

"We do," Jude confirmed. "I'm glad you've been here."

They found Mrs. Ladley waiting at the door, flanked by Lucy Heston and Miss Susan. There were welcoming hugs all around. "Come inside, my dears," she said. "I've got coffee ready, and Maisie's making breakfast. Let's just go to the parlor, shall we?" Her worried eyes betrayed the fact that she was already prepared for bad news. As everyone found a seat, with Jude sitting next to Mrs. Ladley and Lucy Heston on her other side, Delia took a deep breath, knowing one of the most painful parts of their ordeal would take place now.

Gently, Jude told Mrs. Ladley a carefully edited summary of what had happened, that the son she had raised as her own would never be coming home and that her husband was in custody in Fredericksburg and would likely be spending time in prison.

She took the news bravely about Charles, murmuring, "Poor lost soul, poor lost soul…" as she wept. "Oh, Delia dear, I'm just glad you're safe." About her husband, she said nothing at all. Mrs. Heston held her while she cried, and after a few minutes, she and Miss Susan helped her to go lie down in her room.

"Jane and I did a lot of talking while the men were at their meeting last night," Lucy Heston said. "I think she already knew that this was going to end badly for her husband and that boy, and she'd accepted whatever was going to happen. She said she had already decided she wasn't going to join them in Mexico, no matter what."

Over breakfast, Jim Heston told them what had taken place while they were gone.

"After you rode after Delia and Ladley, Jude," James Heston began, "I sent for the sheriff in Mason, and he and a deputy and Doc Jones and I went out to the cave. The Mason sheriff arrested the guards there, and while the deputy was standin' guard over them, he and I went down to the cave and had a look around with a lantern. I'm pretty sure you're right—what I saw embedded in the walls down there looks like pyrite to me. I hit it a coupla whacks with a little hammer I took with me, and it chipped off in crystals, just like you said fool's gold would. There's an assayer on the way to prove it, though—along with the circuit judge to put that pack of scoundrels away for as long as the law allows."

"The rest of them were all still here?" Jude asked, surprised. "Not only the sheriff, but Dawson and Miller and Jeffers, too?"

Heston nodded. "Yup, they were, and wonderin' where the two Ladleys had gone. I think they were just beginnin' to get wind a' the fact they'd been swindled just like the rest a' the townspeople."

Jude and Delia shook their heads in amazement.

"Sheriff Jenkins agreed to testify in exchange for a lighter sentence," Heston went on as Miss Susan and his wife returned to the room. "I called a short meeting the same day, and the whole town was there. Once I told 'em all about the conspiracy, and the fact that both the Ladley men had kidnapped Miss Delia, they were ready to tar an' feather the fellows in jail. But once I told them Dawson said that most of their money was still sittin' in the bank, they calmed down a lot. They're mighty grateful to you, Jude—as I'm sure they'll be tellin' you."

Delia saw Jude duck his head in embarrassment at the praise.

"And that ain't all," Heston said. "Donley Morrison showed up on a lathered nag as we were leavin' the meetin', demandin' Miss Susan go with him—tellin' everyone she was his lawful wife all this time—and the sheriff from Mason arrested him on the spot for bein' an accessory to kidnappin'. He's in the jail with the rest a' the plotters."

"You're safe now!" Delia said to Miss Susan.

"I know," the older woman answered with a smile. "I'm grateful to you for giving me a safe place for so long. I hope you won't mind, but I think I'll be stayin' with Mrs. Ladley for a while. Poor soul, she's going to be so lonely."

Delia assured her she understood.

"I hope you won't mind too much, Jude, but I went ahead and told 'em all you were a preacher," Heston added with an unrepentant grin. "The church board took a vote right then and there and authorized me to tell you the job's yours if you want it."

Jude's face was dismayed. "Jim, there's things I need to tell them that may make them want to change their minds—"

"I doubt it, but they're meetin' early New Year's Eve, so you can speak to 'em then. I'll be there—I've been appointed to the church board to take the mayor's place. 'Course, the sheriff's job is open, too—from the sound a' things, you could take your pick."

"And why don't you be the new mayor?" Jude suggested, only half joking. "As for me, I think I'll do what God wants for a change and be a preacher here, if they'll have me. And Delia's husband, too, of course," he said, smiling and embracing Delia.

"How soon?" Miss Susan asked. "I need a little time to sew the wedding gown, you know. It just so happens I've got some sketches I've been drawing for your consideration, Delia...."

"Is Valentine's Day too soon?" Jude asked Delia.

"Not for me," she said, beaming at him. "Miss Susan, does that give you enough time?"

"Plenty."

Delia gave them all a watery smile. "Is it right to feel so happy when Mrs. Ladley is grieving?"

"She said you'd feel that way, and she doesn't want you to," Miss Susan told her briskly, and Lucy Heston nodded in agreement. "She said Charles threw away his chance at happiness with you, and she was happy that you had found the man who wouldn't ever do that."

Jude pulled her into his arms for a kiss, which left her flustered in front of everyone.

"She also said she wants you to have Zephyr as a wedding present," Mrs. Heston said.

Delia looked uncertain. "She's a beautiful horse and very affectionate, but Jude's right—she *is* a bit too much for me to ride."

"I could work with her," he said. "I've got to admit, I'd been picturing what fine colts we could get if we bred Zephyr to my Shiloh. We could raise fine saddle horses as a sideline."

Delia pondered that. "Maybe we could offer Mrs. Ladley a three-way partnership?"

"Susan, Jim, I think it's time we took these dirty dishes in the kitchen and redded them up," Lucy Heston said, rising and pulling on her husband's hand. "These two have some plans to make, and they don't need a couple of old folks gawking!"

When they were alone, Delia went into his arms, as naturally as a bird returning to its nest. "All I want now is to be your wife—and the very best preacher's wife that ever was."

"Delia, you're the woman God made for me. And that's the best I could ever ask for."

"I like the way you think, Jude Tucker!" she cried, lowering her lips to his for another of his delicious Christmas kisses.

Epilogue

Jude rode on to Delia's house as soon as he left the meeting of the church board on New Year's Eve. They were to have a late dinner, and he would stay until just after the clock chimed midnight and the new year. They would both be glad, Delia knew, when they could begin their married life and he would never have to leave.

"Whew! That Norther's sure made things cold in a hurry," Jude said, coming into the house after he had put Shiloh in the barn. "We may see snow by morning." As if to agree with him, the wind slammed the door shut behind him.

"You're looking at the new preacher of Llano Crossing Church," he told her.

Delia flew into his arm with a whoop of joy. "I knew it!"

He smiled down at her. "It was amazing, Delia. I told them what I'd done in the war, how my faith had been shaken by all the senseless tragedy around me, and afterward—how I'd nearly sinned with that woman—and they said that what mattered was not that I had sinned—we all do, to one degree or another—but that

I'd repented. They all laid hands on me and prayed for me, Delia. I feel so good, so blessed...."

"*We're* blessed, you and I," she said. "What does the board plan to do with the parsonage?"

"They plan to keep it as church property—rent it out for a nominal fee, perhaps, to someone down on his luck. Someday when we pass on, maybe a preacher will live there again."

He kissed her then, and sometime later, she pointed outside. The snow had already begun to fall, and soon the lawn would be white.

"Like a new beginning, the slate has been wiped clean. A new year—in a few hours," she said, as behind them the grandfather clocked chimed the hour. "A new life for the two of us—and for the whole town." She could practically hear her grandpa's—and her papa's—applause.

* * * * *

Dear Reader,

Thank you so much for reading *Hill Country Christmas*. I hope you enjoy reading the story of how sudden, unexpected wealth impacts penniless Delia Keller, and how she learns that people are not always true to the images they project of themselves. Some are better, and some are much, much worse.

With the uncertainty born of growing up poor, without a mother and with a father who did not make his only child a priority, Delia has learned to equate money with security, instead of the Lord. Jude, in contrast, trusted the Lord early, but believed he had gone too far astray to ever serve Him as he did before, or that the Lord would actually provide a good woman like Delia for his wife. I enjoyed writing this story, my first inspirational historical, of how God molds and changes these two, to serve Him and love each other.

I love hearing from readers. You can contact me through my website, www.lauriekingery.com.

Laurie Kingery

Questions for Discussion

1. Have you ever wished to be suddenly wealthy, as Delia is? How well do you think Delia handles it? How well do you think you would?

2. Jude initially discourages Delia's friendliness toward him, worrying it might damage her reputation. What does this tell you about his character?

3. Charles turns out to not be the perfect gentleman he seems to be and Jude reveals himself as not being the rough drifter he seems at first. How reliable do you think first impressions of people are?

4. Do you believe that people who know you would treat you differently if your financial circumstances changed, as Delia's did? Has this ever happened to you? How did it make you feel?

5. Jude believes he has dishonored God by his actions during the Civil War and is no longer worthy to serve Him. How does God show Jude he is forgiven, and that He still wants Jude to serve Him?

6. Charles Ladley has an interesting relationship with his father, Charles Sr. How does it shape his actions? How does the absence of Delia's father shape hers?

7. What happens to change Delia's mind about Jude's character? About Charles's?

8. How different would the life of a young single woman like Delia be if she lived in 2008 instead of the late 1860s? Would you rather live today or in the nineteenth century? Why or why not?

9. Charles and his father and several other town elders try to persuade the townspeople to donate money to a project that would supposedly bring wealth to Llano Crossing. Would you have donated money? Why or why not?

10. Are the people of small towns in America today similar to the people in small towns during the 1800s? How have they changed?

11. What do you think will happen to Mrs. Ladley after the story ends? Will she go on to have a satisfying, happy life? Why or why not?

12. What does it reveal about Delia's and Jude's character that they were willing to stand up for an abused wife such as Miss Susan? How would Miss Susan's life have been different in the twenty-first century?

REQUEST YOUR FREE BOOKS!

2 FREE INSPIRATIONAL NOVELS
PLUS 2
FREE
MYSTERY GIFTS

Love Inspired

LIDIR13